"Has a..."
mouth s...

Pierce mo... ...her provocatively.

Cassie bristled. "I'm calling Polax in the morning to demand he send us someplace else."

"I thought you said you were determined," Pierce countered. "A determined woman stands firm, remember?" His fingers touched her lips. "Not bad. Now if you could just learn to keep your mouth shut...."

"My mouth is what has kept me alive for five years. Most men love my mouth."

"So you talk a man to death, is that it?"

"No. I kiss him to death."

Dear Reader,

Once again EURO-Quest is teaming up with the NSA
Onyxx Agency in book four of my SPY GAMES miniseries.

You met Casmir Balasi in *The Spy Wore Red* as friend and
comrade to Nadja Stefn. At Quest, Casmir is "the actress"—
a femme fatale who is fashion smart, loves sexy clothes and
always gets her man.

I thought it would be interesting to explore what would
happen if a female spy played her game too convincingly
and her target fell in love with her—so in love that he asked
her to marry him. What if during his stint in prison the Red
Mafia Don learned the truth about the love of his life? Add
to the mix a little agency deception, a sexy new partner with
an attitude and a mother with a secret, and suddenly "the
actress" has more baggage than a bride on her honeymoon.

Welcome to Casmir Balasi's world.

I hope you enjoy *The Spy with the Silver Lining*. If the shoe
fits and you're interested in future releases, my backlist, or
missed one of the three previous books in my SPY GAMES
miniseries, log on to www.wendyrosnau.com.

Until next time, remember, it's all in the look, and getting
them to love you. Head up, shoulders straight and never buy
cheap.

Wendy Rosnau

the spy with the
silver lining

Wendy
Rosnau

Silhouette®

BOMBSHELL™

Published by Silhouette Books

America's Publisher of Contemporary Romance

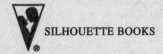

SILHOUETTE BOOKS

ISBN 0-373-51403-4

THE SPY WITH THE SILVER LINING

Copyright © 2006 by Wendy Rosnau

Books by Wendy Rosnau

Silhouette Bombshell

†*The Spy Wore Red* #32
†*The Spy with the Silver Lining* #89

Silhouette Intimate Moments

The Long Hot Summer #996
A Younger Woman #1074
The Right Side of the Law #1110
*Beneath the Silk #1157
*One Way Out #1211
Last Man Standing #1227
†*Perfect Assassin* #1384

Silhouette Books

A Thousand Kisses Deep

*The Brotherhood
†Spy Games

WENDY ROSNAU

resides on sixty secluded acres in Minnesota with her husband and their two children. She divides her time between her family-owned bookstore and writing romantic suspense.

Her first book, *The Long Hot Summer,* was a *Romantic Times BOOKclub* nominee for Best First Series Romance of 2000. Her third book, *The Right Side of the Law,* was a *Romantic Times BOOKclub* Top Pick. She received the Midwest Fiction Writers 2001 Rising Star Award.

Wendy loves to hear from her readers. Visit her Web site at www.wendyrosnau.com.

To Jen
Wise beyond your years, my darling, here's to endurance
and owning who you've become—an amazing young
woman. You've grown with such beauty and grace,
and I'm so very proud.
Love you,
Mom

Chapter 1

The world is a stage, Cassie. Play to your audience and get them to love you. Life is an investment. It's like buying a satin suit and fabulous shoes. You get what you pay for.

Head up, shoulders straight, and remember, never buy cheap.

For twenty-eight years Casmir Balasi had lived by her mother's words, as well as her motto: quality, not quantity. She'd been a trendsetter in her youth, a runway model by age nineteen, and for the past five years Ruza's teachings had turned the blonde with attitude into one of the most valued femmes fatales at EURO-Quest.

Her model figure and fashion sense, along with

her catlike ability to land on her feet, had allowed her to infiltrate some of the most dangerous criminal circles in the world.

Code-named "the actress," she had recovered precious gems, exposed the most cunning criminals, foiled terrorists and carried top-secret documents across enemy lines, while entertaining evil in the process. And each time she had managed to keep her identity a secret to play the game another day.

She'd been as elusive as a grain of sand in a sandstorm. Her top-notch skills allowed her to haul her butt out of tighter spots than a Gucci leather skirt.

Until tonight.

Tonight, the black wide-brimmed Tularo shielding her green eyes and the silver Devicca suit outlining her curves had fallen short. Nasty Nicky was seated at the bar and he was looking straight at her.

Normally that wouldn't have drawn a red flag, but the smug look on his face warned Casmir that he wasn't just enjoying the sight of an attractive woman in a crowd.

There was something else in *that* look.

It was a look of recognition, and something more. As if he knew the secret life behind her secret life.

Casmir scanned the beautiful club, and the throngs of beautiful people who had ventured out tonight to play at the Kelt. If Nicky was here, Yurii Petrov must be somewhere close by. Which meant the Russian had escaped the maximum security prison in Prague where he'd been eating and sleeping, and dreaming of freedom, for the past seven months.

And if that was true, it meant Yurii knew every-thing—who, what and why.

Even more damning, it meant he knew that she was responsible for his recent address change, his dismal room with no view and, no doubt, his weight loss due to crappy prison rations.

She wasn't fool enough to believe that he'd suffered beyond what was bearable. Yurii Petrov had risen to the ranks of *soldato* early in life. He was a hardened criminal who had grown up in the company of hardened criminals. He'd reached Don status to become the most notorious blood-seeking mobster in the Red Mafia.

An iron-tough son of a bitch topped the list on his profile. A detail man who was used to getting what he wanted and holding on to it. A man who didn't blink when it came to following the laws of the cartel.

Had she underestimated Yurii? If he was here, then, yes, she had.

A year ago her assignment had been specific. Trip up Yurii Petrov. Find his weakness and get close to him. So close she knew what brand of toothpaste he used, what made him laugh and what turned him on.

During her research she'd learned why she'd been picked for the job. Yurii had only two weaknesses—apricots from his homeland in Armenia and long-legged blondes.

She'd turned his head within a week, and literally brought him to his knees two months later.

The vision of Yurii on bended knee, pulling a

velvet box from his pocket, flashed in Casmir's mind
and she glanced down at her left hand. She should
never have kept the ring, but it really was beautiful—
a ten-carat marquise diamond set in a circle of
flawless rubies.

"Never take your eyes off your target. That's what
I promised myself that day on the Riviera. Remember, *Kisa?* You were sunbathing topless when I first
laid eyes on your lovelies."

It was Yurii. His Russian accent was thick, his
breath spiked with the familiar brandy-soaked cigars
he favored. His lips brushed the side of her neck, reminding her that they were a little too thin for her
taste. Still, he knew how to use them; after all, he was
the detail man and appreciated perfection in all things.

Yurii captured her hand, spun her quickly, and
suddenly Casmir was looking into a pair of deep-set
earthy brown eyes. He raised her hand and kissed it,
his penetrating eyes locking on the ring he'd given
her months ago.

There was an awkward moment of silence, as if he'd
forgotten what he was going to say. Then he recovered.
"I should be furious with you. But how can I be angry,
my love?" His thumb slowly passed over the diamond
engagement ring on her finger. "You're still wearing
my gift. So just maybe I'll have to rethink killing you."

"Kill your fiancée? Why would you want to? I
thought you loved me, Yurii."

"And I thought the feeling was mutual. But I
heard a disturbing rumor while I was living in my
home away from home."

"Rumors are so unreliable."

"Tell me you didn't set out to betray me, *Kisa*. Tell me it wasn't all a lie. Tell me I didn't let an enemy into my heart, then into my bed."

"I believe the bed came first," Casmir reminded him.

"I remember that night clearly. You were a one of a kind. *Da,* it is why it hurts more than I can express."

If prison had been a hardship, Casmir couldn't tell. Yurii looked fit and healthy at forty-nine, his wavy black hair short, with a touch of gray at his temples just as she remembered.

To go along with his dangerous good looks, he favored black shirts beneath expensive black suits— and always a bloodred silk tie. The picture he presented tonight was a carbon copy of the old Yurii, right down to the scent of his mordant cologne and an imported cigar pinched between his fingers.

Although his five-foot-nine-inch height made him appear more round than lean, his charisma was as powerful as his high-ranked position in the criminal world.

A real sweet deal, is how Ruza would have described him at a glance.

"Deny the betrayal. Let me hear the words from your hot red lips. Lips that have haunted my dreams since we've been apart. Tell me it's all a terrible mistake, my love. Speak the truth."

"I'm wearing your ring. I haven't taken it off since you gave it to me. That is the only truth I know, Yurii."

His hand closed around hers and squeezed. "Not exactly a confession of innocence, my love. Come. We will discuss it in private. My car is waiting."

She felt something hard dig into her side. Without needing to look, she knew Yurii had drawn his Gyurza. The Russian pistol was famous for its cored bullets and penetration ability—a deadly weapon that could go through two sheets of titanium at 100 meters.

Casmir didn't flinch. Instead she glanced left, then right. The nightclub was packed wall to wall, but Pasha had to be there somewhere. A little help from her contact would be appreciated about now.

"If you're looking for your dark-haired friend, I'm afraid she won't be coming. She's met with a tragic accident. A lovely creature, but certainly not you."

If Pasha was dead, Yurii knew for certain that she was a spy for EURO-Quest.

Casmir didn't react to the bad news. She was a professional, after all. She hadn't earned her stripes by wilting under pressure, or spilling tears in the face of the enemy.

She would cry for Pasha later, after she escaped.

Yurii saw betrayal only one way—he would have to kill her.

She had never bought into the cliché that life's a bitch and then you die. Her mother had always professed the opposite—life's a ball, so let's party. Well dressed, of course.

But Yurii wasn't in a mood to celebrate a reunion

in the backseat of his Rolls. She was headed for the Dumpster in the alley, to be picked up with tomorrow morning's garbage. Pasha was probably there waiting for her.

She saw Nasty Nicky slide off the bar stool. He was grinning, his greasy slicked-back red hair bringing more attention to his stubby nose and ruddy complexion.

Someone should suggest a new hairdo to him, and a new wardrobe, too. Double-pleated pants were out, and the cheap fabric had created deep wrinkle lines high on the inside of his sawed-off short legs, making his crotch pooch out like a deformity instead of an endowment.

Yurii's fingers locked around Casmir's wrist. He nudged her with the Gyurza, incentive to head for the exit.

Nicky was now shouldering his way through the crowd to join them. She was out of time. Blood was about to be spilt. Hers, all over her expensive Devicca suit.

Casmir slid her hand into her jacket pocket to retrieve her Makarov. Still playing her lover's game, she turned slowly and poked the barrel of her weapon into Yurii's stomach, just below the safety vest he always wore when he went out in public.

"Feel that, darling? Shoot me, and I shoot you."

He didn't seem surprised by her counter move. Or worried, for that matter.

His smile turned into a shark's smirk. "You really

are a bad girl, aren't you, *Kisa?* One of Quest's most valued she-spies, I'm told."

"If you say so. Now slip your gun into my pocket, or we both die here and now."

"*Da*, a bad bitch."

"A bitch with a gun aimed at your—" she slid the gun lower "—big bad boy."

His grin parted his thin lips, exposing nice white teeth. Yurii was famous for more than his Don status in the Red Mafia; his endowment was as thick as his accent and as penetrating as his Gyurza.

He dropped his gun into her pocket. "So the game begins. I look forward to playing. You know how I love a good challenge, *Kisa*. But in the end we will meet again. You know we must."

"Destiny?"

"Yours and mine. Remember while you're running there isn't anywhere you can hide that I won't find you."

"You're probably right. But you can't blame a bad girl for giving it her best shot. No pun intended."

He released her wrist, brushed her cheek with the back of his hand and ran a finger over her lips. "Extraordinary. From your sexy mouth to your amazing ass. There is no other like you, and even after all the lies I still want you, my love. We are soul mates, you and I. Till death do us part?"

"But not today, Yurii. I would prefer dying a little later. Say…thirty years from now, when my amazing ass has fallen."

Casmir slid her Makarov lower and ran the barrel

over the length of his *big bad boy.* "Dance with me, darling, and keep your hands where I can see them."

Yurii started to move in time with the music. He was a good dancer. A fan of Sinatra.

As they blended into the crowd on the dance floor, Casmir blew him a kiss, then got lost in the mass of gyrating bodies. She reached up and removed her hat. Before the brimmed Tularo settled on the floor, she plucked a few pins, then shook her head, sending the length of her black wig cascading down her back.

She spun right, danced behind a beefy giant grinding his hips. There she pulled her jacket off, quickly turned it inside out and slipped it back on.

Feeling the music, *the actress* danced toward the exit, her silky black hair moving around the shoulders of her shocking pink jacket.

When she wiggled past Nasty Nicky, his eyes never left the dance floor as he searched the crowd for his boss, and the silver goddess wearing the black wide-brimmed hat.

Chapter 2

"You're in the deep freeze, Balasi. Your cover's been blown, and until we can find another use for 'the actress,' and Yurii Petrov is no longer a threat, you're ice."

Four days after her escape from the Kelt in Bratislava, Casmir sat in Lev Polax's office in Prague dressed to kill. She wore a pale-blue satin pantsuit, complete with matching shoes and handbag, her blond hair twisted in a trendy knot, drawing attention to her slender neck and the silver filigree earrings dangling from her ears.

Prepared to sit through her commander's predictable performance—Polax was number one when it came to grandstanding—she crossed her legs and made herself comfortable.

He would do a bit of yelling as he paced the floor, leaving footprints on the plush beige carpet, then stop and yell some more. After exhaustion set in— he was in poor shape, so it wouldn't take long—they would get down to business and discuss the reason he had sent for her at seven in the morning.

"How in the hell did Petrov escape maximum security? That's what I'd like to know." Polax's voice boomed like a cannon. "Now we've got the Russian Mafia crawling up our ass."

It seemed more appropriate to be asking that question to his superiors, or the prison authorities, Casmir thought. She'd done her job. It had taken months to get close to Yurii, and now those months had been flushed down the toilet.

For sure, Quest had taken a giant step backward on this one. Now they would be scrambling to restore their success record in the spy world.

But the really bad news wasn't what Quest had lost, or businesswise what Yurii had lost—his empire was still standing. What he'd lost was far more precious. Far more personal.

"I can't believe this has happened," Polax raged.

Ditto, Casmir thought.

She uncrossed her long legs and played with the diamond on her finger. It really was beautiful. Flawless, Yurii had said. The diamond from Africa, the rubies from Brazil.

Flawless like my future bride, Kisa.

Polax was on his feet now, starting to pace, his pet chair trailing his flat ass. Or maybe it wasn't all that flat. Maybe it only looked that way because his chubby tummy stuck out from his cinched belt like a balloon that had had too many injections of helium.

He stopped and faced her. "Are you hearing any of this? You're sitting there as if you're expecting me to invite you to lunch."

Of course she was hearing him. He was shouting, and as spacious as his office was, the soundproof technology inside created a ping-pong effect. Actually she was hearing everything twice. As far as lunch was concerned it was too early, but breakfast would be nice. A glass of OJ, coffee and a little protein.

"We haven't only lost Petrov. One of our best agents had her throat slit."

It was understandable Polax would be upset about Pasha. She was an excellent agent, an agent who followed Polax's orders to the letter.

Casmir had mourned her comrade in private, the Hungarian with the hot temper. They hadn't always seen eye to eye, but they had respected each other.

Polax was back in his chair, the motorized wonder speeding him behind his monstrosity of a desk.

"The agency can't afford to lose you, too, so pay attention to what I'm saying. I have a plan to defuse this ticking time bomb."

Here it comes, Casmir thought. A new identity on a remote island. Crete sounded nice, or maybe she could spend the summer with Nadja in the Azores. It would be great to see the baby. Nadja had brought Bjorn's child into the world a month ago—a beautiful blond baby boy they had named Dane.

After six months on a tropical beach she'd come back ready to go to work with an amazing tan, as a brunette or a redhead. No, not red, it would clash with her wardrobe. She'd probably have to cut the length. Not her best look, but doable. Gain a few pounds—oh, God, not that.

"I've contacted a friend of mine. Everything has been arranged. You'll leave immediately."

It was time to speak, make a few suggestions. "Someplace warm, I hope. Crete, or maybe I could visit—"

Polax looked over the top of his glasses, which were perched on his puggy, turned-up nose. They were new. Not the best choice for his face shape. Mini oval rims did nothing for his narrow temples. They made his cheeks look like his tummy—as if they had taken one too many hits of helium. A silver finish would have been better than gold, as well. He should have called her and she would have arranged to go with him to pick out something more flattering.

He pulled two passports from his top drawer. "You'll be en route within the hour. No one will know where you are except for me and your bodyguard. He'll pick you up."

"You're giving me a bodyguard? That's generous, but not necessary. I've soloed on more missions than any other agent at Quest. I certainly don't need a babysitter lying on the beach blocking the sun."

"You need whatever I deem relevant. You've been assigned a keeper, and that's that."

"A keeper?"

"If you prefer bodyguard or babysitter, call him what you wish. Watchdog. Glue. Fungus. I don't care." He shoved two passports across his desk. "I hate to inform you of this, but there was a kidnapping attempt on your mother last night. I believe it was initiated by Petrov."

"He went after Mama?"

"If he had been successful he would have used Ruza to lure you out of hiding. You would have probably gotten emotional and made some silly deal with him to free her. Of course that would have ended up with both of you dead. Since that is unacceptable, I've decided—"

"Was she hurt?"

"A bump on the head, and shaken up a bit. I took it upon myself to assign her a guard after the incident in Bratislava. An agent was staked out in front of her apartment. We interceded before she was taken."

"Obviously not a very good one if someone was able to break in."

Another austere look over his glasses. "Ruza is packed and ready to join you on your little getaway. She's been given a story that parallels the bullshit you've been feeding her over the years about working for an international real estate agency. As your real estate boss—" he made a face "—I've told her that we're sending you on a little business/pleasure trip. I sent someone to pack for you. You'll leave straight from here and meet Ruza at the airport."

"Our destination?"

"The U.S."

Too vague. "Where exactly?"

"An out-of-the-way little place called Le Mystère."

"Le Mystère? It sounds lovely. Which coast?"

"The Gulf."

"Florida?"

"Louisiana."

"What's in Louisiana?"

"Alligators, snakes and…hot weather. It seems I've made one of your wishes come true."

"Why not a sunny island in—"

"Because your bodyguard is familiar with Louisiana. He's got a house there."

"With alligators for neighbors."

"Look at it this way. You won't have to make an effort to be…nice. You can be yourself."

At Quest, Casmir was known as the bitch with an attitude, the agent who got away with far more than Polax put up with from anyone else. She didn't know why that was. She knew agents who had been suspended for speaking their mind. She, on the other hand, had simply gotten Polax's famous *look*.

"Does my bodyguard have a name?"

"If I'm not mistaken, you've already met." Polax opened the file on his desk and shuffled through a stack of papers. "Pierce Fourtier was the agent who helped out on the Austrian mission a few months ago. The one you played body double with."

Not that arrogant jackass. No, Casmir thought. The gods wouldn't be that sadistic. Give her anyone else. A seven-foot gorilla with body odor, a three-foot circus midget on crutches. A transvestite with a shoe fetish, and better taste than hers. Anyone, just not Pierce Fourtier.

"An excellent operative. I've never met him, but his file is quite impressive. Seven years as a rat fighter makes him the perfect troubleshooter to watch your backside."

"The perfect asshole, you mean."

"As I said, call him whatever you wish."

"I can't work with him. We didn't get along in Austria."

"I have no record of that."

Of course he didn't—she hadn't made an issue out of it because she was sure she'd never see him again.

"I'm not asking you to like him. You're a professional, and professionals put their differences aside. Bring your acting skills along and you'll do fine. It's always worked before. Until four days ago, that is. This time the only difference will be that instead of standing out in a crowd, and dining with royalty in a two-thousand-dollar miniskirt, you'll be blending in to your surroundings. That should lighten your suitcase, and Quest's expense account."

That was mean. He knew damn well that she spent money out of her pocket for at least half of her wardrobe.

She should point that out. Point her toe and give him a kick under his oversize desk.

Instead, she asked, "How long will it take to put Yurii back behind bars?"

"If I knew that I'd moonlight as a psychic. The important thing is coming out of this smelling like petunias instead of yesterday's socks. The eyes of the intelligence world are watching us. We can't afford to make another mistake where Yurii Petrov is concerned. He'll be out for blood now."

"Mine."

"Well put. He has unlimited resources. Behind every legitimate business he owns there's a million-dollar fraud in the works. From money laundering, to smuggling, to forgery and counterfeiting. He's the go-to man every criminal wants as their friend when they need someone to disappear, or a few billion dollars cleaned. To put him out of business we need the location of his headquarters. It's too bad he never took you there during the months you spent with him."

He was referring to Nescosto Priyatna. Yurii's secret sanctuary was still a mystery to the intelligence world, and to her.

"For us to come out of this bungle with our heads high, we're going to have to get creative. We want his operation destroyed. Until that happens you'll be vacationing in hell."

"Hell?"

"Sorry. I should have said heaven. Snake heaven, that is. I'll keep you up to date on the situation on a need-to-know basis. For now you don't need to know anything, except what time your flight leaves."

"Snake heaven."

"You really are listening. Good."

Casmir knew Quest's policy when it came to offering information—only active agents involved in the mission were briefed on the when, where and how.

She didn't want back in the hot seat, but it was a foolish move to keep her out of the loop altogether. She'd been the only agent to get inside Yurii's tight circle. She knew his habits. Knew things that hadn't made it into his file.

She'd gotten close enough to know that he slept on his back, not his belly. Knew what he did first when he got out of bed in the morning, and it wasn't make a trip to the bathroom. Knew what quenched his thirst above all else, and why he had his shoes custom made, and it wasn't the same reason she did.

She couldn't shake *that* feeling that she always got when the cards in the deck had been switched and she was playing poker, holding a sucker's hand.

She said, "Now that Yurii's been burned, it won't be easy getting close to him. He has plenty of men to do his legwork. Their loyalty is beyond question. And he has Filip."

"Yes, the brother. Thank you for bringing him to my attention." He scribbled the name on a piece of paper. "So that's it, we're on top of the situation, with every confidence that we have the right bait to make Yurii bite."

If they were on top of the situation, Yurii would never have escaped his iron cell in the first place, Casmir thought.

Polax looked up and gave her a satisfied smile. "You're on vacation starting now."

"But I—"

"There's no need to concern yourself further. I'm confident this time things are going to go our way. Get comfortable in your new home and take up a hobby. Knitting, perhaps, or maybe cooking. Can you boil water yet?"

She would like to boil him, and the look she gave him said so.

"You won't be returning to Quest until Petrov's command center has been destroyed and the final paperwork is on my desk. My advice is to put your feet up and enjoy the time off."

"I don't see why—"

"Your argument will be a waste of your time and mine."

Casmir scalded him with her best bitch look. The problem was by now Polax had become immune to it. But she kept it going.

She'd been given the name *royal bitch,* which she embraced. She'd had a good teacher. Her mother had written the rule book on bitchdom, and Casmir had read every word.

A weak woman was as vulnerable as a three-legged dog on a fox hunt, Mama had always said. A strong woman knows how to get what she wants. When to add a cup of sugar, or a drop of arsenic.

A confident woman is wrinkle free, walks like she owns the sidewalk and isn't afraid to kick a little ass when the shoe fits. And if the ass is big, wear boots—preferably a pair you can run in should your aim be an inch or two off and the brute doesn't go down.

Polax was speaking again. Casmir made eye contact, her eyes snapping like a bitch on fire.

He dismissed the look. "We never know what tomorrow will bring in the intelligence business, Balasi. Four days ago you were *the actress*. A busy little spy doing what you do best, playing games with a winning hand. But now your cards have been turned over and Petrov knows you outplayed him. Until we have him back, you're—"

"A prisoner with an asshole jailer."

"A jailer who has a reputation that gives new meaning to the word survival. I'm confident Fourtier will be able to protect you should your sunny disposition irritate the neighbors and start them hissing."

Very funny, Casmir thought. If a reptile crossed her path, she was going to shoot it in the head with Yurii's dependable Gyurza. She still had his gun, with a round of ammo guaranteed to turn Fourtier's neighbors into leather shoes, complete with matching handbags.

"Your plane is waiting, and so is your mother. I'm sure Ruza will recover from her injuries in a few days."

"Injuries. But you said—"

"The minor bump on the head and black eye haven't slowed her down much."

"Mama has a black eye?"

"In a few days she'll look as beautiful as ever. Now get going."

"But—"

"Your flight leaves—" Polax checked his watch "—in fifty minutes. Move your amazing ass, Balasi. I'll be in touch."

* * *

Pierce entered Merrick's office at Onyxx in Washington expecting a pat on the back, and his vacation request confirmed. He and Jacy had managed to wrap up the kill-file mission and defuse a time bomb.

All was good, and now it was time for a little fun in the sun. He deserved it. He was anxious.

"Sit down, Pierce. That was a helluva job you did for us in Montana. Jacy's back working for us. Polax is happy that Prisca has joined his team of female spies. And we have the original kill-file in our possession."

"And Holic Reznik?"

"Holic is never going to see the light of day. His prison cell at Clume is now his permanent home."

"And the Chameleon?"

"We've alerted the appropriate organizations directly involved in his intended mayhem. Of course, we still want him, but for now lives have been spared. You and Jacy can be damn proud of that. The agency is grateful."

All in a day, Pierce thought. Now let's settle on a date when I leave for my requested time off. He probably wouldn't get a month like he'd asked for, but surely two weeks. He could live with that.

"Sorry to have to tell you this, but your request for vacation time has been denied."

Pierce had just sat down. He looked across the desk at his commander in disbelief. He hadn't had time off in over a year. Not unless they were counting his recovery time from taking those two bullets for

Bjorn in Austria months ago. Rehab had been no picnic, but he'd gotten used to the routine. He had more bullet holes in him than all his teammates put together. Still, a little rehab hardly qualified as a vacation.

"You're denying my request? Why?"

"Polax called and he's got a problem."

"Since when are his problems our problems? Or should I say, mine?"

"When they parallel our interests. He's uncovered a critical piece of information, and that information could put us back on the trail of the Chameleon. Ever hear of a man named Yurii Petrov?"

"The Russian mobster, *oui*, I've heard of him. He's doing time in a Czech prison."

"Was. He escaped a week ago."

"How the hell did that happen?"

"I don't have all the details. What I do know is that since he's been in prison his operation has still been running smoothly. We know he's the prime source for laundering the Chameleon's money. Last week someone pulled off a billion-dollar weapons deal with the Russians. We believe it was the Chameleon."

Pierce shifted in his chair and crossed his jean-clad leg over his knee, his frustration in check.

His comrades had given him the name Sleeper years ago because he seldom showed an ounce of emotion, or revealed what he was thinking. His self-control was what had kept him alive for thirty-five years. His lazy brown eyes gave the impression that even if his balls were on fire, he wouldn't reach for a water glass.

He said, "You think he's going to contact Petrov to clean his money?"

"He probably already has. Polax tells me Yurii Petrov keeps sophisticated records on all his clients. That means he's got data on the Chameleon. We want it."

"Do we know where Yurii Petrov keeps this data?"

"We think he has a command center somewhere in the Mediterranean. But so far we haven't been able to lock in on the location. To infiltrate his core and retrieve the data we need to uncover his hideout. He calls it Nescosto Priyatna. Quest has been under some heavy ridicule since Petrov's prison break. Polax is looking to redeem his agency. We're looking for data on the Chameleon. I've met twice with Lev Polax and we've come up with a plan."

"If you don't know where to look, how are you—"

"Petrov has a score to settle with Quest. Polax believes he's going to go after one of his operatives. The agent responsible for his seven months in prison."

"How do I fit in?"

"When agencies work together good things can happen. The Austrian mission was proof of that. I've never been too proud to join forces with another agency if we can score a victory. Shutting down Petrov's cartel would be a big perk for EURO-Quest. And I don't have to tell you what it would mean to Onyxx if we can draw the Chameleon out of hiding to get another crack at him."

Pierce could see that the idea thrilled Merrick. And why wouldn't it? The Chameleon had been a dagger in Merrick's side for fifteen years. This went far beyond just business with his boss. Everything involving the Chameleon was personal to Merrick.

"We've got the Chameleon's original kill-file now. We've defused an international disaster and made friends along the way. It's a victory, but what I…Onyxx wants is the Chameleon. I'd like to have been there when he learned that we had commandeered his kill-file. That bastard has been dogging me…the agency for too damn long."

It was a fact, and Pierce understood Merrick's frustration. His commander had been living with a sour taste in his mouth for too long. After all, the Chameleon had killed Merrick's wife.

"I'd like to nurture this neighborly relationship with Quest. It's been working to both our advantages." Merrick tossed a file across the desk. "This is what we've got on Yurii Petrov. He's a leading force in the Red Mafia, but he's much more than that. He's been a busy man over the past twelve years."

Pierce reached for the file and opened it. First off was a picture of Petrov, along with the stats. Five feet nine inches, weighed two ten, brown eyes, black hair. In the picture he was dressed like a tycoon. He looked in good shape for a man headed for fifty.

He skimmed the pages of information. Later he would read them through. He closed the file.

That was when Merrick dropped the bomb. "What I want from you is to play house with Polax's bait. It's only a matter of time before Petrov makes a move on her. How long has it been since you were back home?"

The question caught Pierce by surprise. "Home? You mean Louisiana?"

"Le Mystère, to be specific."

"Four or five years, maybe."

"How's Saber Lazie doing these days?"

Pierce arched an eyebrow. "He's still on his feet, kicking it around."

"So you two are still on good terms?"

"Oui." Where was this going?

"You still have that house near Bayou La-fourche?"

Pierce uncrossed his legs and sat up a little straighter. "What are you asking of me, Merrick?"

"This is a bodyguard job with a twist." Merrick slid another file across the desk. "Polax's agent. The one you'll be playing house with until Petrov makes his move. She comes with baggage."

"What kind of baggage?"

"Her mother."

Pierce reached for the second file and opened it, and there staring back at him was the mouthy little bitch he'd encountered months ago in Austria. The woman he'd been tempted to shove out of the heli-copter if only one of his bullet wounds hadn't dislo-cated his shoulder in the process.

He closed the file. "Balasi put Yurii Petrov in prison? How did she manage that?"

"She used her charm. You know the standard for

Quest agents. They're trained specialists in the art of seduction."

The woman he'd met didn't know the definition of charm, Pierce thought.

"This particular agent is an expert in bringing a man to his knees. Polax tells me Petrov fell in two months. So hard he declared his love, gave her a ring and asked her to marry him."

Casmir Balasi, wife material? A two-headed viper would be more fun.

"This isn't going to work." Pierce closed the file. "We didn't get along in Austria."

"Then you know her?"

"She was the agent that doubled for Nadja Stefn that day in Austria on Glass Mountain."

"If you had a conflict with her, why isn't it in your report?"

Because he had never expected to ever see her again, Pierce wanted to say. He didn't. Instead he made a suggestion. "Maybe Ash Kelly could take this one. I hear he's been back a few weeks."

"It's true Ash has returned from his sabbatical. He seems a hundred percent, but I'd hate to find out otherwise on a mission of this importance. To be honest, he never made the list of candidates. After I discussed potential operatives with Polax, he picked you as the lucky winner."

Pierce muttered under his breath.

"What was that?"

"Indigestion."

"This mission will require a man who can stay

focused and in control." Merrick grinned. "We both know you have a knack for that. You've proven to us more than once that you can straddle an electric fence in a knife fight and never break a sweat. That's your gift, Pierce—patience and adaptability. Not to mention your dead aim. I've never seen a man who can keep a cigarette lit in the eye of a hurricane better than you can. How many times have you been shot now?"

"I've lost count."

"My point. It's that resilience that I'm counting on."

Bad weather, he could handle. Eating a bullet, no problem. But babysitting a bitch with more attitude than brains... He'd volunteer for a bullet in the middle of the Arctic any day.

In his entire thirty-five years no one had been able to get under his skin the way Balasi had. If he was forced to do this, he was the one who was going to need an extended sabbatical...in a padded cell.

He asked, "What's up with the mother? How does she fit into this?"

"There's an interesting story behind Ruza Balasi. She's somewhat of a legend in Europe. A retired stage actress. Polax tells me Yurii Petrov tried to kidnap her a few days ago. He wants her to vanish for a while. That's where your friend Lazie comes in."

"Is she another hurricane?"

"Excuse me?"

"You know the saying. Like mother, like daughter."

"In this case, more than you know. Polax shared

some interesting facts with me. A little history I wasn't aware of. Want to hear more?"

"If I say yes, does that lock me in?"

"You were locked in the moment Polax took a look at you, then read your file."

"I'm still not sold on the idea."

"You've got what it takes to pull this off. I know it, and you do, too. It's not going to be easy, and it might not end up picture perfect—rarely do missions go as planned. But I'm in agreement with Polax. You're the man. One more thing. When this is over, Casmir Balasi must be alive. If she's not breathing air, you and I will be facing a firing squad, along with Polax. That's no bullshit."

Chapter 3

"Oh, Mama, your eye… Does it hurt?"

"Of course it hurts."

"It looks…ghastly."

"Thank you, Cassie. I feel so much better knowing that we both agree I look terrible."

They had left Prague's Ruzyne Airport on a commercial flight headed for the U.S. Ruza was dressed all in black. As usual, her silver-gray hair was neat and glamorous, twisted into a low knot at the nape of her neck, secured with a diamond clip.

Casmir always admired the fact that her mother looked stunning no matter what. Black eye and all, at age fifty-two, Ruza Balasi was a vintage classic. She knew what color looked best to complement her flawless complexion, and what to eat to keep her slender five-eight figure below 120.

Her mother slipped her sunglasses back into place. "Is this going to remain a surprise or are you going to tell me where we're going? I haven't taken a vacation with you in years. I'm looking forward to some extravagant shopping, and dining out every night."

Casmir settled into her seat, contemplating how to tell her mother that their vacation spot wasn't going to be a sandy beach in the Mediterranean, or a shopping extravaganza in Paris.

"This is a work vacation, Mama. I can't play the entire time."

"That's fine. Just point me in the direction of the most expensive dress shop and I'll be happy."

"My boss said—"

"Such a nice man, Mr. Polax."

Casmir raised her perfectly arched blond eyebrows. "Yes, isn't he. Definitely one of a kind."

"We like one of a kinds, don't we, dear?" Ruza patted Casmir's hand, then eyed her daughter's scarf. "Is that a Naubow?"

"Yes."

"I thought so. There is nothing that compares with French silk. And these colors…they're so vibrant. You really do look good in saguaro green and salmon. You should wear them more often."

"What did you pack, Mama?"

"Not what I would have liked. With only one good eye to guide me through my wardrobe, I fear we'll have to do some major shopping right away."

From what Polax had told her, shopping was going to be a bit of a problem. How to tell Mama they were headed for the swamp, their babysitter a snake named Mr. Asshole?

Casmir continued to contemplate, then decided to hold off. Something ingenious would surely come to her in the next few hours.

Mama believed that Quest was an international real estate agency. Casmir would never have considered lying to her mother if she had thought she could handle the truth. But there was no way Mama would have understood. Her first question would have been, "Is it dangerous?"

After all, she was the offspring of Madame Ruza, a retired stage actress who ate fruit and salad to keep herself trim, and visited the beauty salon for a manicure and pedicure weekly. She enjoyed grand parties and sipping martinis dressed in negligees trimmed in fur with matching satin bedroom slippers.

College had bored her, and her runway modeling career had grown stale. But she had honestly never been bored a day in the five years since she'd worked for Quest. She'd come to accept that her present life had been one of those fated twists in the road. Who would have guessed she'd become a spy the day she had bumped into Polax on the street?

"On this trip I'm going to be inspecting a number of properties for an interested client," Casmir began. "Property in Louisiana."

"We're going to the U.S.?"

"Yes. Louisiana."

"There's this decadent place there that I've read about. It's called New Orleans. Wouldn't it be grand to go there?"

"We're flying into New Orleans."

"Oh, this is so exciting."

"Le Mystère," Casmir added. "The place where we'll be staying is called Le Mystère. I think it's farther south."

Pierce flew into New Orleans, then rented an open Jeep. The city brought back memories, and he found himself driving by the Glitterbug. He'd been a bartender there during his lean and mean years. Later, when Saber Lazie had felt he was ready, he'd graduated to the underground game room where real money could be made.

A den of muscle, guts and killer instincts, was how Saber had described the place when he'd first opened the door and Pierce had gotten his initial look at what Lazie's twisted mind had designed below the Glitterbug.

After a few lessons from the master himself, he had stepped into a world that quickly separated the men from the boys. Before long he'd made a name for himself, and enough money to buy some land and build a cabin. A money-making job and regular meals—it was perfect for someone like him.

Then he'd met Merrick. The Onyxx commander had been seated in the front row one night. He'd sat at a table alone, his eyes never leaving the action. Days earlier Pierce had agreed to a high-stakes knife fight with a muscle-honed giant named Frog.

The win had been one of his toughest, but he'd managed to stay on his feet, and eventually become the winner of five thousand dollars.

The victory had put him at Merrick's table hours later. The commander of Onyxx had bought him a drink, then laid his cards on the table. He said Pierce was a desirable candidate for a government special-ops team. He'd complimented him on his skill and survival techniques, saying that he was one of the best he'd seen anywhere, and that he'd been everywhere, so he should know. That there was a place for men like him.

The truth was Pierce had always felt alone, that there would never be a place for a man like him. But here was a stranger telling him he had value.

Merrick had sweetened the deal with a money figure that Pierce couldn't have made in his entire lifetime. And so he had become one of Merrick's boys. A man of purpose, one of the elite at Onyxx.

He didn't stop in the Glitterbug, but he saw that it looked the same as it always had from the out-side—a simple hole-in-the-wall bar, complete with strippers and loud music. It was a lucrative business for Saber Lazie, but he'd made his real fortune ar-ranging fights underground.

The door was open, as always, welcoming the regulars and the curious. But few knew about Lazie's exotic other world, or how much money changed hands in one night.

He glanced at the files in the seat beside him, still skeptical about the job. Bodyguard with a twist... This was a twisted mess, all right. Merrick hadn't been kidding when he detailed the plan that he and Polax had come up with. He was supposed to keep Balasi hip-huggingly close until Petrov took the bait.

He wanted to put off his face-to-face meeting with her as long as he could, so he'd called Lazie to talk over the situation. Even though he was in New Orleans and could have picked up his cargo at the airport, he had persuaded his old friend to do the honors.

Besides, he had some catching up to do. There was someone he wanted to see in Le Mystère first. It had been four years since he'd seen sweet, generous Linet at the Ginger Root.

Lazie said she still worked behind the bar, serving beer with a smile. Keeping that picture in his mind, he headed south, bypassed Chalmette and followed the river.

He took Highway 39 to Scarsdale, then Stella. Thirty minutes later he cruised into Le Mystère. The main street was quiet, as usual, with two cars parked in front of Pete's Grocery, one in front of Wanda's Catfish Lounge and nine in front of the Ginger Root Bar.

Linet must be working, Pierce thought as he swung into the bar's dirt-packed parking lot and hopped out. He hoped that Linet would be happy to see him. It would make his stay in Le Mystère more enjoyable if he had a little diversion from time to time. A small black-haired distraction with green eyes, and a set of wanna-touch-me breasts that had kept the bar stools at the Root covered from dawn until dusk for the past twelve years.

It was a known fact that some of the boys staked out a bar stool early and stayed all day and all night just to be on the receiving end of one of Linet's boob-a-licious smiles.

Today Pierce planned to be one of the boys. He needed to get into the right frame of mind to face hell in heels.

It would take at least a dozen beers, maybe more.

It was said a man's worth was measured by degrees of talent, skill and determination. Yurii Petrov had been born with a full glass of all three.

Once a simple Caucasian peasant from the mountains of Armenia, he'd first found his calling with the Russian Mafia. As a member of *the family* he'd fit the mold like a well-made shoe.

His penchant for detail and his gut-driven loyalty had sent him climbing the ladder quickly. And for his efforts he'd become a very rich man. No, a stinking, filthy rich man.

Over the years he'd perfected his skills, put his money where so many men put their mouths and quickly learned the advantages of becoming number one at everything he attempted.

Laundering money was a worldwide business, a lucrative business. But to do it flawlessly, without a trace, was an art form.

Yurii was an artist.

It had taken years to develop his faultless system, years to capitalize on the weaknesses of foolish businessmen and the greed that often followed misguided power. But he'd been patient and true to his calling. He'd watched and learned, and made his move time and again, until he'd turned millions into billions.

It had set him apart from the ordinary criminals who daily shuffled a few thousand in and out of banks and nightclubs. He was now considered the kingpin in the world of turning dirty money into street currency.

His life had been a wild ride to the top. There had been women along the way. Nights of hot sex and excess. But he'd always woken up empty.

When you least expect a miracle, it comes riding on the back of something wonderful. His mother used to say that to him and his brothers when they were kids.

He'd never expected *Kisa* to be that something wonderful the day he'd seen *her* lying on the beach on the Riviera. But suddenly, at forty-nine, with money falling out of his pockets, respected by his peers, and a thriving empire, he had found what was missing in his life—he'd fallen in love.

Power and wealth paled in comparison when a man had found his soul mate. And for a short four months he had been happy beyond his wildest dreams.

Kisa was perfection, her scent like a smothering flower, her voice the long-awaited aphrodisiac to the road of serenity. And when he first kissed her venomous lips, he'd been eager to be stung by her poison, willing it to infect his soul.

It had all been so perfect, and then he'd learned the truth about the woman he'd seen as his destiny.

For months, he'd lain awake at night in his prison cell thinking about how he would kill her. He had planned for it, dreamed of it. And then he'd seen his ring on her finger in Bratislava.

Why was she still wearing his ring?

Maybe the idea of snuffing her out of his life would grow on him again, but for now killing *Kisa* was the furthest thing from his mind.

Yurii closed his eyes and tried to imagine his hands around her neck, choking the life out of her.

He fed his muse, but it was no use. He wanted his life back. The life she had given him.

He wanted his *Kisa* back.

And maybe, after a time, his feelings for her would grow cold, and once his heart had become a chunk of ice, the idea of killing her would bring more comfort than torment.

He would think on it, but first there was business to attend to. It wouldn't take long. He wasn't crazy about a rendezvous in the middle of the Mediterranean with the Chameleon, but he was more than simply a good customer.

The Chameleon was a man much like himself. He was a man of honor and power. A family man with a wife and a son. He valued his home, and his privacy in the Greek Isles.

He had no need to know exactly where. And like-wise, there was no need for anyone to know where he sought refuge away from the eyes of the world.

Da, a rendezvous at sea with the Chameleon, a few words exchanged. Dates and times agreed upon. A price settled. The deal sealed over a drink and a handshake. Then he would be free to focus on *Kisa.*

He understood now why a powerful man bitten by love broke the rules. *Nyet,* he was not weak. He was a realist. Or maybe a better word was a fatalist.

Kisa was his fate.

And he, hers.

Yurii smiled as he thought about their meeting at the Kelt in Bratislava. He could have killed her easily. He could have slit her throat as Nicky had done to the brunette with the big tits. But he had wanted to hear her sultry voice once more, and touch her satin-smooth skin. Smell her sweet scent and taste her perfect lips.

And then he'd seen her finger weighted down by his gift.

He remembered the day he'd given her the ring. Afterward they had made love. The memory aroused him and he laid his hand against his cock and pressed hard as he pulsed to life.

He felt himself stretch as his blood began to hum through his veins. He worked his hand up then down, envisioned *Kisa* undoing his pants and taking him in her hands. His fingers would get lost in her hair as she knelt to cover him with her mouth.

He groaned, felt himself on the verge of ejaculation. He let it come where he stood on the balcony outside his lavish bedroom overlooking the lagoon.

Confident no eyes were watching him, he succumbed to his fate. The fate of a woman who had tricked him. A woman he should hate.

A woman he still loved.

The phone rang minutes later, and Yurii glanced down to see which button had lit up. It was Nicky, and he hit the intercom.

"What news do you have for me?"

"She flies across the Atlantic. Recovery will require a trip to the U.S."

"Where exactly?"

"I will have the location very soon."

"*Spasibo,* Nicky. You know what to do."

"Your instructions are clear. Anything for you, Don Petrov."

Yurii pressed the button to disconnect, then picked up the cigar that smoldered in the ashtray on the balcony ledge. Puffing hard, until the air turned gray and pungent, he stepped back and disappeared inside his bedroom to take a shower.

Chapter 4

"He was supposed to meet us," Casmir said as she eyed the throngs of people coming and going at New Orleans International Airport. "That would be just like him to be late picking us up."

"Who, Cassie?"

Casmir caught herself before she said, the asshole. "Pierce Fourtier, Mama. A coworker. He's taking us to Le Mystère."

"A coworker? I don't recognize the name. Have I ever met him?"

No, but once you do you'll never forget him, Casmir thought.

She spied a gypsy vagrant watching them and immediately she went on red alert. No one was supposed to know their destination but Polax…and Fourtier, of course. No one should be singling them out of the crowd unless…

She couldn't dismiss Yurii's last words as she'd skipped away from him at the Kelt four days ago— *so the hunt begins. I look forward to it.*

She pulled her mother toward the door.

"Where are we going, Cassie?"

"Out, Mama."

They had already gone to the baggage claim and picked up their luggage. Since then, they had been waiting for Fourtier a long thirty minutes.

Bastard.

Casmir looked over her shoulder and saw the gypsy was still eyeing them. No, he wasn't only staring, he was moving through the crowd toward them with a confident swagger, his long gray hair defying his age, as well as the fit of his jeans.

He wore a sleazy red satin vest over a black shirt, and he was also sporting a tacky long earring dangling clean to his jaw.

Someone should clue him in on how to dress when you're over fifty, she thought. Playing Bojangles wasn't working for him—not at all.

Where the hell was Fourtier?

He probably had stopped off somewhere for a beer.

Casmir ushered her mother out the door and into the busy crowd that waited for taxis. She slipped past the mass of bodies, pulling her luggage behind her. Her mother followed, dragging her Paris tote, her dark glasses still in place hiding her black eye.

Casmir spotted an unmarked taxi parked across the street. The driver was leaning against a silver SUV and smoking a cigarette. None of the tourists had spotted him yet.

She bolted into the street, waving her hand to get the rebel cabby's attention. He jumped to attention the minute he saw her and hurried to meet them. She thrust her bag at him, and yanked the Paris tote from her mother and heaved that at him as well. Shoving her mother into the backseat, she followed after her and slammed the door shut.

"Are we in a hurry, Cassie?"

"Do you want to stand in the heat, Mama?"

"I've never been able to tolerate it, you know that. Goodness, it's warm. I had no idea. This reminds me of the jungle in—"

"Jungle? What jungle, Mama?"

"There, you see, the heat is getting to me already. I don't know what I'm saying."

Casmir felt a little dizzy herself. The air was as thick as sand inside the cab, and twice as suffocating.

She kept watch out the window as the driver tossed their luggage into the trunk. She spotted the gypsy as he burst through the crowd just as the cab-driver climbed behind the wheel.

"We're in a hurry," she said. "Step on it."

As the cabby sped away from the curb, Casmir watched the gypsy jog into the middle of the street, his feet lighter than she'd expected for a man his age. When he pulled a phone from his pocket, she knew she had guessed right. He was one of Yurii Petrov's henchman—the hunt *was* on.

The first thing on the agenda was to lose the gypsy. Once they accomplished that, she would phone Polax and tell him that their ace bodyguard was a no-show, and that Yurii had somehow found them.

Then she would demand a sandy beach in Crete with a breeze, and that Fourtier be hung from a low tree over an alligator pond in his backyard.

Pierce answered his phone on the forth ring. He was straddling a bar stool at the Ginger Root, enjoying his fifth beer and Linet's assets as she made eyes at him from across the bar.

"Lazie, you pick up my package?"

"We got a problem, boy. *Da* two of *dem* took off. I'm chasin', but *dat* sonofabitch cabby's got a lead foot and two glass eyes. He's *gonta* end up turned over in the levee if he keeps *dis* up."

"What the hell do you mean, they took off?"

"Like a jackrabbit with his tail on fire."

"What made them run? Didn't you tell her who you were?"

"Didn't get close enough ta introduce myself, *mon ami. Dey* slipped away like a greased snake on a spit run."

"Where are you now?"

"In *da* Eldorado playin' Starsky and Hutch."

"Don't lose them. I'm heading back." Pierce disconnected and jammed the phone in his pocket.

"Sorry, honey, but we're going to have to continue this reunion later. I got a rabbit to run down."

Linet pouted. "Let's hope it *don* take another four years for you ta get back here, cowboy. If you still look as good *outa dem* jeans as I remember, there's no reason you shouldn't be sharin' the bounty. In the south, sharin' is the neighborly thing ta do. *Oui?*"

Pierce grinned, then winked. "I'll be back."

"You know where I'll be, cowboy."

He left the Ginger Root and started back to New Orleans with his foot pushed to the floorboard, while he pulled his cell phone and called Lazie.

"You still got them in sight?"

"Not at the moment. Got a corner *ta* take."

Pierce heard tires squealing. Lazie swore in colorful French. "What's happening?"

"Got *um* back. Shit, lost *um* again. I'm *gonta* rattle that cabby's cage when I catch him. Call *yous* later. Got another corner *ta* take."

Pierce tossed the phone in the seat next to him. It would take him forty minutes to get back into town. He should never have sent Lazie to the airport. Merrick had said the plan would take time to set into motion—that the heat wouldn't be on for at least two days.

He should have known that where Miss Bitch was concerned, the heat was never off.

Pierce stewed all the way back to the city until he was well cooked and starting to burn. He picked up the phone in the seat next to him as he crossed the river and punched in Lazie's number again.

"Update me."

"Caught the cab. He's bleedin'. He says he let *dem* out on the corner of Bourbon and St. Anns. *Dere* in the Quarter somewhere. That's a good sign."

"You lost them."

"I got *dere* luggage."

"I don't give a shit about their luggage. Meet me at the Bug."

Casmir pulled her mother into a dingy bar on Bourbon Street, then wished she hadn't. The seedy establishment was sporting a topless dancer on a spotlit stage and a clientele that was ninety-nine percent male. The only female in sight was the redhead grinding her hips on stage and sporting a red thong and a smile so wide you could count her teeth.

She spotted an empty table in a dark corner at the back of the bar. It wasn't the most desirable spot for hungry eyes bent on viewing every dimple and mole on the redhead—the reason it had been left vacant, no doubt. But it was a perfect rest stop for two women on the run and out of breath.

"Over here." Casmir took Ruza by the hand and led her mother along the wall to the secluded table. "Sit down, Mama."

Her mother was still wearing her dark glasses and she stumbled into the table and almost knocked it over. The noise turned heads and suddenly two dozen smiles acknowledged the arrival of the female duo.

Casmir took a head count, then assessed the grins.

Oh, goody. This was just what they needed. A room full of depraved lechers to add to their problems.

"This is just great," she huffed.

"I agree." Ruza sighed. "My shoes are killing my feet. It's been years since I cruised the streets in heels."

"What?"

"Never mind. I'm just glad to finally sit down. I think I've got a blister on my toe."

Casmir took a seat beside her mother. She kept one eye on the entrance, and one eye on a man ten feet away who hadn't stopped grinning since they'd found the empty table. She pulled her phone from her pocket, then just as quickly stuffed it back when the man and his friend stood and started sauntering toward them.

"Stay put, Mama, I'll be right back." Casmir met the men halfway. Before they got a chance to say anything, she said, "We're meeting our fellas, boys, so don't get excited. They'll be here in a few minutes and my boyfriend is a real jealous badass. We just want to enjoy a drink in quiet while we wait."

One of the men nodded—the big burly one. But there was an asshole in every crowd, and Big Burly's long-haired companion was it.

"Come on, *cher.* I'll show you a better time *den* your boyfriend. I got more experience *den* a dog's got hairs on his ass."

"I'm sure you do, but I'm into the tall, dark, silent type. And did I mention manners? A lady values manners and…good hygiene. Not hairy assholes."

"Ain't no ladies come in here, *cher.* None *dat* I *knows* can talk like *dat.*"

While they had been in the cab, Casmir had slipped her Makarov out of the secret compartment in her purse and into her jacket pocket. She came up with it and nudged the crude dog in the ribs.

"Sometimes it's hard to distinguish the difference, but you're going to have to take my word for it." She gave him a solid poke with the barrel of her gun. "Or not. It's your choice."

He glanced down, saw the gun. His eyes doubled their original size. "Hold on, lady…"

"That's right…lady. I thought you'd come around. Now go sit down and do your barking at the stage."

When they walked off, Casmir returned to her seat, her gun neatly tucked back in her pocket. Keeping her eyes out for incoming trouble, she concentrated on cooling off.

"The air-conditioning in this place must be broken," she said.

"What did you say to those men, Cassie?"

"I just told them we wanted to enjoy our drinks… alone."

"Drinks? That sounds absolutely wonderful. I could use a Russian Rose."

Her mother had removed her dark glasses. Casmir stared at Ruza's black eye in the dim light. She was worried about her mother. She had to get her someplace safe.

She pulled out her phone. "I don't think a martini

is a good idea right now, Mama. At the moment we need to keep our wits about us."

"My wits are always sharpened after a martini. Even better after two. When I get to number three—"

"I know what happens after number three, Mama. If you need to lie down in here, you could start a riot. No martinis."

"But I've acquired quite a thirst, Cassie. We've seen half of the city from the backseat of a taxicab, and we haven't been here an hour. That cabdriver must have been on speed. Did you see how many red lights he ran? And what about our luggage?"

"I need to make a phone call."

"To Mr. Fourtier?"

Never, Casmir thought. Not even if she was stranded in a snake pit with an alligator gnawing on her ankle. "I'm calling…my boss. Are you going to be all right sitting here for a few minutes?"

"Of course. About our luggage…"

"Later, Mama." Casmir got up and rounded the table. There was a hall with a flashing sign above it indicating the restrooms. "Don't move from this table. Do you hear, Mama? I want you sitting right here when I get back."

"I don't think I could move if I wanted to. Don't worry. My butt is glue."

Pierce walked through the front door of the Glitterbug at the same time as Lazie came through the back door. His jaw was set, but Saber—who was used to the shit hitting the fan on the hour—was wearing a wide grin. His old friend was in his element when he was knee-deep in sewage digging for treasure at the bottom.

They met at the bar. "Good to see you, *mon ami*. It's been a while. You're lookin' fit for a man in bed with the government. At the moment it looks like your mood could be better—" he shrugged "—but women can have that affect on a man, *oui*. We'll find *dem*, no worries."

"We better or Merrick is going to send me to Greenland naked to count snowflakes. You said they took off when they saw you?"

"*Dat's* right. Say, who's *da* hot cookie *dat's* with your lady? I ain't seen nothin' *dat* shiny and sweet in years."

"That's the mother." Pierce ignored Lazie's goofy grin. It was rare to see Saber in a bad mood, even when a bucket of shit was raining down on his parade. Only this time it was *his* parade, and Merrick wasn't going to be happy if he learned he'd lost the bait out of the starting gate.

He said, "You take this side of the street, and I'll take the—"

"Cookie!"

"What?"

Lazie had turned around to lean against the bar. He was looking out past the crowd of men who had come to enjoy the afternoon strip show. Pierce turned his head, and there in the far corner of the room sat an attractive woman in her early fifties.

"Is that Balasi's mother?"

"It is, *mon ami*." Lazie's grin widened. "What did you say her name was?"

"I didn't. You sure that's her?"

"*Dat's da maman.* And look, she's a spirited *ange,* too."

Pierce watched as a waitress set a martini down in front of the woman.

Lazie put his hand over his heart. "I'm in love, *mon ami.* Tell me *mon coeur's* name?"

"Snap out of it, Lazie. Ruza Balasi isn't your type."

"Ruza-a…" Lazie let the name hang on his silver, Southern tongue. *"Ma douce amie."*

"She's not your love." Pierce scanned the room looking for Casmir. "She wouldn't leave her mother," he muttered, thinking out loud. "No luggage. On foot. Strange city. What would she do? *Oui,* I know. She'd make a call to Polax."

The music was loud and the catcalls the stripper was getting added to the noise. Pierce glanced at the hall leading to the restrooms, thought a moment.

He grabbed Lazie by the front of his shirt. "Get your eyes back in your head and your mind off your dick. And put your hand down. It looks like your having a heart attack."

"Mais, yeah. It's true. My heart has been attacked by Ruza-a…"

"One of these days I'll enlighten you about sweet Ruza Balasi, but right now this is what you're going to do."

Pierce leaned close and whispered his plan into Lazie's pierced ear.

* * *

Ruza sensed a pair of eyes watching her. She shoved her dark glasses to the end of her nose and scanned the room. There, at the bar. It was the shady-looking character who needed a haircut.

As he began to swagger over to the table, she wondered what was taking Cassie so long. She wasn't up for conversation with a stranger. She was simply too exhausted.

She took a gulp of her martini to fortify the upcoming confrontation.

"*Oui,* a fine-lookin' woman, Cookie. A classy *maman,* who looks like she's lived a life of experience, no?"

"It's true," she answered. "I wasn't born yesterday, so before this gets awkward, I'll say no, thank you. Now run along."

"*Oui,* a spirited *maman.* I enjoy a woman who can teach an old dog a new trick on all four."

Ruza lifted her glass to her lips again. "Well, Mr. Dog, you must have a hearing problem. I said, run along."

Instead of moving off, he chuckled. "So you like my place, do you, *mon coeur?*"

Ruza removed her glasses, momentarily forgetting about her black eye. "I have no—"

"*Ma douce amie,* you've been injured. Who has hurt you, my sweet? I'll kill the bastard."

She arched her shapely gray eyebrows above her damaged eye. "You said you're the owner of—" she looked toward the stage "—this cheap acting den?"

"*Oui.* The very one. Saber Lazie at your service, *mon coeur.*" He pulled out a chair and sat. "I haven't seen you here before. Have you come to my city on business or seeking pleasure?"

"That would be my business."

Another chuckle. "*Oui,* a spirited woman, with a snake's bite. The man who hurt you, does he still have his legs?"

She studied him a moment, got a whiff of his cologne, but couldn't recognize it. It smelled familiar. That was odd.

"All you need to know—Lazie—is that I'm not ripe for plucking. I'm waiting for my daughter. You're sitting in her chair. As you can see, I've bought a drink from your lacking establishment, so I'm not loitering."

"Ruza-a…do you dance?"

"How do you know my name?"

He stood. "It's a fittin' name, for one so lovely. I like slender women, and memorable names. You're a feast for a man's eyes and his imagination."

His sharp eyes drifted to her chest.

Ruza considering going for the mace in her handbag, which lay on the table. Not yet, she thought. He still hadn't explained how he knew her name.

She emptied her martini glass, then asked again, "Who told you my name?"

He shrugged, checked his watch. "It's time to go."

She saw him step around the table. Then his hand

was on the back of her chair. With a sudden jerk he pulled it way from the table, and then lifted Ruza off her chair and tossed her over his shoulder. It happened so quickly she had no time to react or reach for her mace.

The bar crowd was too busy watching the stage to notice Ruza being carried out the back door. She began to pound her fists into his kidneys as he stepped out into the back alley.

Screaming, she fought harder, but the man was stronger than he looked. He ignored her blows as he rolled her inside the trunk of the car parked next to the building.

"*Don* worry, Cookie. I'll let you out soon."

Then he slammed down the trunk and the car's engine roared to life.

Ruza started to scream again. Maybe someone would hear her. That hope turned to dust as the radio speaker inside the car began to vibrate and drowned out her cries.

The car sped away as Aaron Neville began to sing "Use Me."

Oh, God. Lazie—if that was his real name—was going to assault her, then kill her.

Worse, at her funeral she would be sporting a black eye.

Chapter 5

Pierce stopped next to the women's bathroom and pressed his ear to the door. He'd guessed right. She was on the phone, chewing off Polax's ear, and anything else that was dangling unprotected.

"Fourtier never showed at the airport. And Yurii has already found us. One of his men was at the airport. Send someone to get us out of here. Pierce Fourtier is not only an asshole, he can't tell time, either. If he'd picked us up when he was supposed to, that gypsy scum with the earring might have missed us loitering in the lobby. I want a new contact, and a new location. And you can tell your pal from Onyxx that I want Fourtier on his knees licking up garbage with his tongue for the next month."

Pierce slowly turned the doorknob and slipped inside. He saw a pair of blue stilettos and slender ankles in the end stall.

He locked the door, walked to the last sink in a line of three and perched his backside on it, aligning himself with the door she was behind. Arms crossed over his chest, he lit a cigarette and continued to listen and learn what she *really* thought of him in between a few choice adjectives.

Minutes later he heard the toilet flush, and then Miss Bitch opened the door and stepped out, wearing a blue satin pantsuit.

"Lick up garbage with my tongue?"

"You… How did you get in here?"

"Not on my knees."

She started for the door. Pierce slid off the sink and followed. When she tried the door and found it locked she spun around.

"You've been fired, so get off my back and stop breathing down my neck. Polax is sending someone dependable to pick up Mama and me."

"I'm not off the job until I've been notified by my boss, and until then you're my baggage." He saw her hand disappear into her pocket. He grabbed her wrist, raised his arm and pinned it to the door. He dropped the cigarette to the floor with his other hand, and while it died a slow death, he said, "Your first mistake was running from the airport. Your second is trying to pull a gun on me."

"I wouldn't have had to run if my ride had showed. What was I supposed to do, let Petrov's gunman stuff us in a trunk and drive us to the nearest landfill? Whatever plan your boss and Polax cooked up is a joke."

"And you think I'm a joke, too?"

"If the shoe fits, buy a pair in every color."

He could snap her beautiful neck so damn easy. Instead, Pierce backed off. After all, he was the calm and collected one, while she was the spitfire who never knew when to shut up.

She turned, unlocked the door and walked out. He followed, stopping in the hall to light another cigarette. He took his time, taking a much-needed drag of nicotine. As he entered the bar, he saw her head for the table where she'd left her mother.

She picked up the empty martini glass, then turned to search all four corners of the bar. When she didn't see Ruza anywhere, she spun a half turn and nailed him with that bitch look that had made her famous in the spy world as one of Quest's untouchables.

"Where's my mother?"

"How should I know?"

"Because you're a—"

"*Oui*, I know." He sauntered to the table, sat down in a chair. "The words you used on the phone when you were burning Polax's ears were, a useless turd in a sea of stink."

"Where is she?"

"Sit down."

"I said—"

"Sit."

She hesitated, then jerked the empty chair out, and as she sat, she slammed the empty martini glass down between them. "Okay, I'm sitting. Where's my mother?"

"On her way to Le Mystère."

"With who?"

"The gypsy scum."

The gypsy wasn't one of Yurii's loyal *soldatos*. Casmir contemplated that. Rationalized why it had been easy to make the mistake. Considering the man's appearance at the airport, it had been an easy one to make.

"And where were you when we got off the plane, riding in the gypsy's pocket?"

"I sent Lazie to pick you up in my place."

"Without telling me? Why would you change the plan and send a new contact? Someone I didn't know or expect? I'm confused."

"Use that line when you call Polax back. Tell him you got turned around and you made a mistake."

He had to be kidding. "The mistake was yours, not mine. You never showed at the airport, and now some wild vagabond wearing an earring has hijacked my mother. She's probably scared out of her wits."

"Make the call."

"I have a better idea. You make a call to the gypsy. Tell him to bring Mama back."

"That would be a wasted trip. We'll be joining them soon enough."

"I'm not going anywhere with you. Besides not being able to tell time, you don't hear well, do you?"

"You want to see Mama, right? Lazie's got quite a reputation as a lady's man."

"Somehow I'm not worried Mama is going to fall hard for your colorful friend unless it's while she's scrambling to get downwind. He probably smells as bad as he looks."

"Lazie has never been above taking what he wants when his mind is set."

"You're not suggesting that his mind is set on having my mother?"

"He did confess an interest in Cookie."

"Cookie?"

"He's already given her a nickname. *Sweet,* isn't it?"

Casmir narrowed her eyes. "Are you blackmailing me?"

"*Oui.* Call Polax."

"No."

"Tell him you ate something on the plane that scrambled your brain. Tell him since you last talked, you've taken some antacid, and now you're thinking straight. Tell him we're together and things have worked out."

Casmir was so busy plotting the appropriate death for Mr. Asshole that she didn't see the guy she'd had words with earlier leave his table and head their way.

"Your jealous badass boyfriend finally show up, *cher?*"

She looked up and saw the cretin she'd backed off at gunpoint. Big Burly was once again behind him—the giant looked like barroom brawling was his profession instead of his hobby.

Whatever, Casmir thought, but he really needed to get himself some new friends and a haircut and invest in a new razor.

"I asked if *dis* is *da* boyfriend you was crowin' about, *cher?*"

She had never had a boyfriend, but if she was ever in the market for one, Pierce Fourtier wouldn't make the bottom of the list. He was arrogant, practiced deviant tactics and no doubt had the morals of a rodent. Which was probably why Onyxx had recruited him as a rat fighter.

She glanced at Pierce, who had lit another cigarette—she added chain smoking to the list of his unsavory behavior—then looked back at the cretin who didn't know when to give up.

"How old are you?"

The question seemed to throw him. He blinked his bloodshot eyes, then slowly grinned. "Old enough to know what *ta* do with you, *cher.*"

Casmir rolled her eyes. "What's your name?"

"Name's Parnel, sweet thin'."

"Well, Parnel, I'm surprised that someone hasn't shut you up permanently by now. If this is your routine every time a woman comes through the front door, I'm amazed that your throat hasn't been slit, or your kneecaps blown off."

Pierce chuckled, and Parnel gave her *boyfriend* a narrow-eyed glare. "You tough enough to slit my throat, badass?"

"It could happen, *mon ami,* if you're not out of my face in five seconds."

"You think you've got big enough balls to send me to hell?" Parnel grabbed his crotch. "I guarantee mine are bigger. I can back up what I say in an alley or in the bedroom."

His friend stepped up and gave Parnel an elbow. "You've made a mistake. This guy is—"

"Shut up, Frog."

"You should listen to your friend. He knows something you don't. Something you don't want to find out the hard way."

Casmir glanced at Pierce, then Parnel's muscle-bound friend, who had just been given the name Frog. An interesting nickname, but Big Burly fit him better.

Pierce and Frog exchanged *that* look. The look of recognition. Parnel never saw it: he was too busy puffing up his chest.

"I *doan* like you. I'm not so sure I like your girl-friend anymore neither, but no one tells me *ta* get lost. What's it gonna be, fists or knives?"

"Parnel, I'm tellin' you, this guy isn't someone you want to piss off."

"Stuff it, Frog. He's *da* one who should be worried 'bout pissin' me off."

"But you don't want to fight him. He's—"

"I said, shut up. We can do *dis* outside, or right here. Winner goes home with blondie."

"Ha!" Casmir laughed, knowing full well that Pierce Fourtier would never agree to such a ridiculous wager.

She watched him stand. Now she would get to see just how tough Pierce really was.

She studied his stance. She had to admit that he really did come off as a hard case. He had attitude, as well as a lean and fit body—the best in the bar from what she'd seen so far.

Okay, so he wasn't bad looking, either, but that didn't mean she'd changed her mind about his growing list of faults. He was still out of a job, because she was never going to call Polax and go willingly to Le Mystère.

With his expression composed, and his dark eyes giving nothing away—she remembered that about him in Austria—he said, "Your five seconds are up. I choose knives. Location, downstairs. Frog, set it up. By the way, it's good to see you again, *mon ami*. It looks like Lazie's been treating you well."

Casmir leapt to her feet. "Are you crazy? No one bets me in a wager. I'm not some—"

Pierce slipped his arm around her and pulled her against him. "Have faith in your boyfriend, *amant*. If I lose, what is one night with Parnel?" He gestured to the man, who was now grinning like an idiot. "Look, he has all his teeth, and he's guaranteed you a pair of big balls. What more can a woman want in a man?"

Parnel's grin grew while Casmir's anger doubled. She tried to pry his hand off her hip. When that didn't work, she finally found her voice and hissed in his ear, "Let go of me or your balls are going to be in your throat a second before I kill you."

Her threat didn't seem to worry him, or budge his hand. He said, "I'll join you in an hour." When the two men walked off, he looked at Casmir. "You want to see Mama, *oui*? Killing me won't make that happen, but it will give Lazie a chance to be alone with Cookie overnight."

"More blackmail."

"Blackmail? Fact? You make the call."

"What's downstairs?"

"A game room."

"What kind of game room, and how do you know about it?"

He let go of her. "I used to work here."

Curious now, seeing that he was serious, she asked, "How good are you with a knife? Do you think you can win?"

"Worried about me?"

"I'm worried about finding Le Mystère after dark to rescue my mother from the gypsy should you end up a slab of meat at the morgue."

"I'm thirsty. I need a beer. You? What's your poison, *amant*?"

"Call the gypsy and warn him off. Tell him—"

"His name is Saber Lazie, and Cookie will be fine as long as she doesn't do anything stupid. It takes a lot to piss Lazie off."

Mama would be too afraid to do something stupid, Casmir thought. Still…

"He better not lay a finger on her or he'll be wearing another piercing. Only this hole will be bigger. Straight through his chest."

"Somehow I believe you would do it."

"The first intelligent thought you've had all day. You don't have to fight Parnel. We could leave now, and—"

"We? You've changed your mind about calling Polax and bailing?"

She hadn't, but he didn't need to know that. "Maybe. It all depends on you and how quickly we can get out of here. Shall we go?"

"What kind of boyfriend would I be if I didn't fight for my *amant*? If I ran like a *tcheue*?"

"No one here would think you're a chicken, Fourtier. You look more like a snake. And you're not my boyfriend. I only said that to get Parnel to back off."

"And did he…get off your back?"

"Not right away. He needed a bit more persuasion. But in the end—"

"So you shoved your gun up his nose and told him to eat it, didn't you?"

"Stomach, and only after he insulted me. I wouldn't have had to get nasty if he'd known when to walk away. Why does every man think that a woman is just supposed to roll over and drool when he snaps his fingers?"

"Not every man. I like my women moaning, not drooling. Not as messy, and better for the ego."

"A bodyguard with a sense of humor. Who would have thought a snake would have a funny side? They're so one-dimensional."

"This snake is a barrel of fun once you get to know me."

"No, thanks."

Grinning, he headed for the bar. Over his shoulder, he said, "Coming?"

Scowling at him, Casmir followed and slid onto a bar stool. She had expected him to do the same, but he stepped behind the bar and slapped the man tending customers on the back.

"How's it going, Lute?"

"I never expected to see you back here, Pierce. You come to visit Lazie?"

"Something like that. I'll wait on the lady."

The bartender nodded. "Sure, *mon ami.* You know your way around. *Nuttin's* changed."

"Sometimes that's a good thing."

"*Oui.* Like a steady paycheck and sex twice a week with my old lady. Always look forward to Tuesdays and Fridays. A man's routine is his best friend."

The man named Lute gave Casmir a sweet grin before he moved to the end of the bar to wait on another thirsty customer. She dismissed the short little man with shaggy brown hair, and focused on Pierce Fourtier.

"Now then, *tite chatte,* you want a real drink, or something pretty?"

"I don't think I should be drinking."

"Does that mean you can't handle your liquor?"

"I can handle whatever you throw my way. I could drink you under the table if necessary."

His reaction to her boast was another healthy chuckle. She noticed straight white teeth, and mentally listed them under fit body, nice nose and clear complexion. Okay, so she'd noticed his nice skin, along with a pair of soul-deep brown eyes.

"We'll have to settle that one of these nights. See who can outlast who."

"Then you plan on taking me to Le Mystère?"

"*Oui*. There was never any doubt."

Okay, this was the way it was going to work. She'd go with him, get Mama and leave two minutes later.

Casmir started to stand. "Let's go."

"After I meet Parnel downstairs."

She sat back down. "What if you don't win? I don't think we should jeopardize Mama's safety for ego's sake, do you?"

"Lazie won't let anything happen to Ruza." He reached for a bottle of vodka and began to mix her a drink. At least she suspected it was hers. He'd said he needed a beer.

Using all the tools of the trade, and knowing where to find whatever he needed, he produced a martini glass and poured the mix into it from a shaker and set it down in front of her.

"There you are, *amant*. A fitting drink for Quest's *actress*."

"What is it?"

"The house special. The Glitterbug's version of a French Kiss."

"You used to be a bartender here."

"*Oui,* one of the best in New Orleans." He popped the top off of a beer and raised it in the air. "Here's to patience, and adaptability. He that has patience, can have what he will."

He recited poetry. She would never have guessed that. She answered, "How poor are they that have not patience. What wound did not heal but by degrees."

He raised his beer bottle a little higher. "To Franklin and Shakespeare. And to survival. Let's hope by the time this is over one of us hasn't killed the other."

"You don't like me?"

"About as much as you like me, *amant.*"

After all she had survived on her travels around the world, dying in the trunk of a car on foreign soil held no appeal.

Ruza wished she had her purse. She needed a mint to soothe her raw throat from too much screaming. The mace would have been a good thing to have about now, too.

She felt around in the darkness. The trunk was empty, not even a tire iron.

An hour later the car stopped. Ruza closed her eyes and waited for her kidnapper to open the trunk. She lay still, as if she'd been overcome by exhaust fumes. Not far from the truth.

"Come on, Cookie, wake up."

She didn't move. Waited until she could feel him draw closer. Until the smell of his cologne told her he'd stuck his head inside the trunk. She recognized the scent now. It was Duperau. Impossible, she thought. In Russia the cologne cost a small fortune. This man didn't look like he could afford toilet water straight out of the pot.

"Come, *mon coeur.* Let me help you."

Keying on the direction of his voice, Ruza squinted open one eye, sized up her assailant, then doubled up her fist and gave him an uppercut straight to his jaw.

He staggered back, leaving a mere two-foot opening for her to escape the trunk. Ruza scrambled out just as he was getting his balance back. That was when she aimed her foot and kicked him in the crotch.

"Bon Dieu, mon coeur," he groaned.

He bent forward, grabbing his box of jewels, and when he did Ruza doubled up her fist once more and gave him another punch. When he dropped to his knees, she turned and ran.

She got ten yards when she noticed her surroundings. Nothing but tangled foliage, woods and water. Dear God in heaven, the gypsy had driven her to the ends of the earth.

Ruza realized her only escape was the road. That would require stealing his car. She rounded the Eldorado just as the gypsy staggered back to his feet. She was reaching for the door when he made a wild dive at her.

Knocked off balance, Ruza was taken out like a football quarterback a yard from the goal line.

"No!" She began to fight like a cat attacked by a bulldog. She scratched and clawed, tried to raise her knee to his crotch. She gave it a good effort, but the gypsy was a resilient advisory.

Pinned on her back, he grinned down at her.

"Careful, Cookie, when we get *ta* know each other better you might want *ta* use *dat*. It would be a sad day *if'n* I couldn't perform up *ta* your expectations because of a little misunderstandin' on our first date."

"I assure you there has been no misunderstanding, you lout. You accosted me and stuffed me in the trunk of your car. If that's what you call a date you're as crazy as you look."

"I was only followin' instruction, *mon coeur.*"

That took the fight out of her. "Whose instructions?"

"Your daughter's."

"My Cassie would never hire someone to kidnap me, or stuff me in a trunk, Mr. Lazie. You're not only a kidnapper and a lout, you're a liar. Now get off me before I scream."

"That would be a waste of energy, Ruza-a.... There is no one to hear you but me."

She tried to toss him off, squirming like a bagged fish beneath him.

Willing to ride out her anger on top until she tired, he moaned, "*Oui,* Cookie, I have found my match. A vigorous woman, soft in all the right places."

"You're making a deadly mistake, Lazie. Get off me, or die."

Her threat didn't faze him. She squirmed some more until she felt him growing against her belly. Oh, God, she was polishing his jewels. No wonder he was grinning.

"Now look what you've done, Cookie. You've awakened the dragon."

"I've done nothing of the sort, Lazie."

"Does that feel like nothing, *mon coeur?*"

The fact that she had turned him on sent an alarming shiver throughout Ruza's slender body. She didn't recognize it for what it was at first—it had been years since she had felt sexually hungry. Not since Jacko, Cassie's father.

The very idea that this stranger had awakened her and trespassed on Jacko's memory enraged her. Those emotions were sacred, and she protested the moment with a fit of screaming.

"*Bon Dieu,* Cookie…my poor ears."

It was the last thing he said before Saber Lazie took Ruza's face in his hands and shut her up with a kiss, unaware that he had trespassed further on sacred ground.

Chapter 6

When Polax called, Merrick was on his way home from his office. Alone in his black Corvette, he reached for his private phone inside his jacket pocket.

"You have an update already?"

"Not an update. More like a new problem. Are you clear to talk?"

"Go ahead."

"Your man didn't show at the airport, and Balasi is on the run. She claims Petrov is already hot on her heels. I thought you said Fourtier was reliable."

Merrick slid in and out of traffic as he contemplated Polax's news. "Pierce is a damn good operative. If he didn't show there was a good reason. I'll find out what that is and call you back."

"Do it immediately. Balasi isn't happy, and while I'm not in the business of soothing ruffled feathers, she is the key to pulling off this mission. I was candid with you about everything. Balasi is more than just a sexy spy. She has to come out of this on top. I thought I made myself clear on that."

"You did, and I understand completely."

"When she called she demanded I fly her and Ruza out of there. She also wants Fourtier's hide tanned and turned into a pair of shoes."

"I'll check out this recent glitch and call you back."

"I'll be anxious to hear how Fourtier explains not showing up at the airport. It better be damn good, or I'll personally buy those shoes and wear his hide."

When Polax disconnected, Merrick swore, then punched in Pierce's number. When Pierce didn't answer his phone, Merrick swore again. He'd wait an hour and if he still couldn't reach him, he would have to recruit another operative to follow up on the situation, because Polax was right. They couldn't afford for anything to go wrong.

He had meet IsaDora, the head of Quest, only once, and she had made quite an impression. She wouldn't have approved this mission, and for that reason they needed to keep her in the dark until this was all over.

That meant Pierce better get Casmir Balasi turned around in a hurry. If that required a little ass-kissing, he'd better pucker up.

* * *

Casmir descended the stairs into a secret world she couldn't have dreamed up with a hit of cocaine and a whiskey chaser.

She had been in gambling dens from Istanbul to Cairo, human action houses in Singapore. She'd even spent some time in a harem in the Arabian desert. But she had never seen a gaming den like this one.

Beneath the sleazy bar was an island of concrete surrounded by water. A game room was what Pierce had said. There were four ten-foot-wide levels that circled the arena, each level lined with tables and chairs where the spectators could drink, make wagers and cheer on their favorite fool.

Casmir took in every aspect of the deadly playing field as Pierce nudged her forward.

"Nothing to say?"

She turned and glared at him.

He returned a grin. "Over here, *amant*. You can cheer on your boyfriend from the front row."

He took her arm and led her up six steps to a table. Surrounding the first level was a three-foot railing. The black filigree iron rail had been installed to keep the onlookers from toppling into the water—though if you had a death wish you could easily climb over it to play double jeopardy with the reptiles she now saw waiting for their next meal to drop.

He said as he seated her, "A front-row seat for a woman used to being in the middle of the action."

"This is crazy. You're actually going to fight Parnel out there?" She pointed to the fifteen-foot-square cement slab that rose out of the water four feet.

"That's right."

"Why?"

"Why not?"

When she had no answer for him, he took a step back and peeled off his brown T-shirt. She had secretly admitted that his body was fit, but now she could see that what she'd first thought was above average was honed perfection—every muscle he owned defined and accounted for.

Okay, so her appreciation of his body rose a few more notches. That didn't change the fact that he was a reckless ass who smoked too much. And there was also a question of brains—if he thought there was nothing wrong with this playing field surrounded by alligators, he was past crazy.

The knife sheathed on his belt caught her eye. It wasn't an ordinary knife. It was longer, with a curved handle. Casmir had seen a number of unusual knives in her day, handled a few herself, but this was far different than anything she'd seen.

Frog appeared across the water. He was standing on a man-made concrete shoreline holding on to two suspended ropes.

He raised his hand. "*Mon ami,* are you ready?"

"*Oui.* And your mouthy little friend?"

"Parnel might talk too much, but he's not a coward."

"Too bad for him."

Casmir watched Frog let go of one of the ropes.

The thick coil sailed across the playing field and Pierce reached out and caught it out of the air.

He looked back at her. "A kiss for good luck, *amant?*"

"How about a promise instead? If you're not back here in twenty minutes, I'm leaving."

He checked his watch, blew her a kiss, then reached a little higher on the rope and let it lift him to the railing. Balancing like a man who'd been born in a circus, his muscles flexed and straining, he swung himself over the water and dropped onto the raised slab of cement.

He had just landed when Parnel appeared next to Frog and took the second rope. Like Pierce, he was wearing only jeans, his feet sporting leather boots. She quickly glanced at what Pierce was wearing for foot gear. It looked like he was wearing slippery-soled cowboy boots.

Great. He would fall on his ass within seconds and be gator bait a minute later.

She found a seat, watched as Parnel extended one of his legs as he sailed through the air toward Pierce. He was going to kick Pierce off the slab before the fight ever got started.

She knew what she would do. She'd been trained by some of the best martial arts experts in the spy business. She watched Pierce spin right and, at the same time, reach out and grab Parnel's foot in midair. He gave it a jerk and Parnel lost his grip on the rope. The move wasn't pretty, but it was fast and his opponent landed hard on the cement slab.

To Parnel's credit, he quickly rolled and scrambled back to his feet, pulling a knife sheathed at his hip.

The blade was long and it looked like something meant to gut one of the reptiles that were now circling the concrete slab. He flashed the knife as if taunting Pierce with it. Then he lunged forward and lashed outward, but the blade only caught air as Pierce jumped back.

Casmir expected to see Pierce reach for his knife at that moment. She waited, but he never went for it.

"What are you waiting for?" she yelled down at him. "Pull your knife out of your ass!"

He turned his head in her direction, and in that second Parnel struck, taking advantage of the distraction. He lunged forward, this time drawing first blood—catching Pierce high on his muscular arm.

He was bleeding like a stuck pig, but he never even flinched. Instead he spun in a tight circle, then kicked outward as he came around, planting his foot in Parnel's stomach. The force lifted Parnel off his feet and he flew a good eight feet and landed on his back, close to the edge of the slab. Stunned, he seemed unable to get up.

Pierce was on him within seconds. He grabbed Parnel's wrist, forced his weapon to fall out of his hand, then dropped his knee onto his chest. Suddenly a hungry alligator surfaced and Parnel must have caught sight of it. He started screaming and flaying his arms, begging for Pierce to let him up.

Casmir had no idea what Pierce would do next. Seconds turned into a long minute. Finally he lifted his knee. She could see that words were being exchanged, then Pierce stood, grabbed one of the ropes overhead and swung back to her, dropping blood over the water from the gash on his arm.

He reached the railing and, still holding on to the rope, balanced on it as he loomed above her. He looked like a warrior back from the battlefield.

When he let go of the rope and dropped down beside her, Casmir didn't say anything. She was at a loss for words.

He looked at his watch. Said, "Six minutes to spare."

"Why didn't you use your knife?"

"Because it would have been murder. Parnel's a novice. I need a better reason to kill a man than stupidity." He glanced at the blood covering his arm. "Next time, *amant*, keep that pretty mouth of yours shut. You're enough of a distraction without it."

He turned and gave an upward nod to Frog, who was now helping Parnel to his feet. Then he took hold of her arm and lifted her off the chair.

She'd taken half a dozen steps when he said, "I guess I'm the winner of the prize. It looks like you're going home with me."

Pierce was on his way to Le Mystère with Casmir seated beside him in the Jeep when his phone went off. He reached for it between the seats and put it to his ear.

"*Oui.*"

"I got a call from Polax and he tells me you didn't pick up Balasi and her mother at the airport. What the hell's going on? She's—"

"Right here beside me."

"They're both all right?"

"Oui."

"She told Polax that Petrov has already located her. Is that true?"

"No. It was a case of mistaken identity."

"Then everything's back on track?"

"Oui."

"So I can call Polax and tell him the plan still stands?"

"Oui."

"You can't talk?"

"Oui."

"Call me later."

When Pierce disconnected, Casmir said, "Was that Merrick?"

He glanced at her. She looked like she was sucking on a lemon. In Austria she'd had a similar look. Casmir Balasi was used to things going her way. But not this time. He was in charge of this mission, and it would be handled his way.

He intended to share pieces of the operation as needed, but not right away. He said, "It was Merrick. You need to call Polax."

"And tell him I was wrong."

"You were wrong."

"You didn't show at the airport. I wasn't wrong about that."

"Petrov doesn't know where you're at. Polax needs to be assured of that. Mistakes were made. Let's just—"

"Your mistake, not mine. I was forced to do what I had to do to survive. That's what I was trained to do. And I had my mother to think about."

"Enough, *amant*. Let's just pull it back together for the sake of the mission."

"Mission?"

"Wrong word. Vacation."

"This is hardly a vacation."

"See, we're starting to agree already."

"I won't let this go so you can look good at Onyxx. You're the one who screwed up."

"When you get to know me better you'll find out I don't give a damn about how I look. I do what I do, and I live with the outcome."

"Typical man."

"What's that suppose to mean?"

"You're the smart one, you figure it out."

This was going to be hell, Pierce thought. He would surely strangle her before week's end.

"Can we bury the hatchet?" he asked, keeping his voice level and as emotionless as possible.

"Where do you want it? Skull, or a little lower? What do you value most? I'll be sure to take that off first."

"This is bullshit." Pierce slammed on the brakes and pulled to the side of the road. He put the Jeep into Park, then reached across her and swung open the passenger door. "Out."

"What?"

"You heard me. Out. I'm done."

"Done?"

"Done with you. Call Polax and tell him any damn thing you want. Tell him I left you stranded. Tell him I quit. Tell him you need a new bodyguard. One who's deaf."

They were on a back road about three miles from Le Mystère. His home was another two miles farther south. He looked down at her feet. If she took off her shoes, and dug in her heels, she could make it in to town before dark.

"And Mama?"

"I'll send her into town with Lazie. If you stay on this road, you'll find it. Your kind always manage somehow."

"My kind? What's that suppose to mean?

"You're a smart girl, you figure it out," he said, tossing her words back at her. "Now move your ass."

"No."

Pierce swore, then climbed out of the Jeep. He rounded the hood and reached into the passenger side to haul her out. She had to know what was coming. Maybe that was why she pulled her gun on him. He never expected it, had been too pissed off at the moment to remember that she was a resourceful bitch.

"Back up."

"Or you'll shoot me?"

"That would be murder. I need a better reason to kill a man than stupidity." She tossed more of his words back at him, then aimed the gun at his right leg. "But knocking you down a notch wouldn't cause me any sleepless nights. Doubt it?"

Pierce knew he'd made a rare mistake. She was dead serious about shooting him. Not ending his life, but he'd go down nonetheless. He backed up, watched as she reached out and slammed the door shut, then climbed over the console and into the driver's seat.

Then she was speeding away from him, leaving him on the side of the road in a cloud of dust.

He realized a moment later that his cell phone was still in the Jeep. He couldn't even call Lazie to come get him.

"Sonofabitch."

It was the beginning of a long string of crude adjectives as Pierce dug in his heels and started toward Le Mystère. Five minutes later, he flagged down Murphy Logen on his way in to Le Mystère to sell his daily catch of fish to Wanda at the Catfish Lounge.

He was a fool if he thought she was going to let him quit. No one quit on her unless it was her idea.

I'm done. Ha!

He would be done when she said he was done.

Casmir rounded a corner and saw what looked like a town. If this was Le Mystère, Mama was going to flip out. Shopping in this town, unless it was for gas and groceries, was definitely out.

She spotted a bar that seemed to have more activity than anyplace else and pulled the Jeep into the dirt parking lot in front of the Ginger Root. Hoping that someone in this godforsaken place would know the address of Pierce Fourtier's home, she stepped through the front door and scanned the dingy bar.

No surprises inside: it was a carbon copy of the outside, even though the handful of lightbulbs dangling from the ceiling defused a multitude of sins. It smelled like a smoker's heaven. A place Pierce would probably like, she thought.

She scanned the crowd of men collected at the bar, looking for someone Pierce would know—another gypsy scum. There were several to pick from.

She headed for the empty stool at the bar, noting there was a woman serving the crusty clientele—the only woman in the place besides herself. She was a dark-haired woman who looked to be in her thirties. A little on the short side, but what she lacked in height, she made up for in curves.

Casmir had always been self-conscious of her slight bustline, and the point hit home as she eyed the brunette's cleavage. She wanted to blame the endowment on the woman's pink two-sizes-too-small T-shirt, but fair was fair.

"What can I *gittcha?*" the busty bartender asked.

"I'll have a…" Casmir glanced down the length of the bar as she perched herself on the stool. "A beer, I guess."

"On tap I got—"

"Anything will be fine."

The woman stared at her, as did the men lining the bar. It was no doubt due to her European accent.

"You lost?" the woman asked, setting the glass of beer in front of her.

Casmir reached for the glass. "I need an address," she began.

"An address?"

"Yes, a street address."

That brought forth a few chuckles.

"We don't got no street addresses around here. All the mail is dropped off over at Wanda's. You a foreigner?"

"I'm not local."

"That's obvious, honey. You're lost, right?"

"Not exactly."

"Then why do you need an address?"

The woman's frank questions set Casmir to thinking. Polax had told her to blend in to her surroundings. It was clear she would never fit in here. Not unless she lost an eye and grew a wart. She hadn't given it much thought until now, the disguise she would use to *fit in.* But by the looks she was getting she needed to come up with something fast.

"I'm meeting my boyfriend. He lives around here."

That statement raised every eyebrow at the bar. Not able to take it back, Casmir produced the best suck-up smile she could muster. That was something she didn't need to think about. The actress could charm the pants off a guard at Fort Knox.

"Who might that be?"

The question came from the end of the bar. Casmir stretched her neck and locked eyes with a shabbily dressed man in a ponytail wearing a leather strap around his neck with a knife dangling from it half the length of his arm.

She hesitated, glanced down at her hand, and suddenly the perfect cover popped into her head. "My boyfriend, or maybe I should say fiancé, is from around here." Casmir spun the diamond and ruby ring on her finger to bring attention to it. "His name is Pierce Fourtier. Ever heard of him?"

The minute she dropped the name the entire room turned quiet. She glanced at the woman—whose mouth had dropped—then down the line of vagrants straddling their stools. Her perfect cover suddenly didn't seem so perfect—they were all looking at her as if she'd lost her mind.

"You're saying Pierce is your man?" Miss Bosom asked.

A second later the line of beer drinkers burst into laughter.

Casmir opened her mouth to speak, but before she could get anything out, the door slammed and all eyes turned to see who had walked in. She followed suit, and there stood Pierce, looking as if he wanted to kill someone.

If she didn't do something quick, he was going to ruin her perfect lie and her perfect cover for being in Snake Heaven. But then, would that really matter? She wasn't going to be here that long. If she found Mama by dark, they could be gone by morning.

She stood, checked her smile, then, making sure

her acting skills were in play—an excited bride-to-be—she rushed to Pierce and wrapped her arms around his neck and planted a kiss on his lips before he had time to slit her throat.

Chapter 7

She had shocked him, then went to work on the kiss until he kissed her back. Casmir knew how to put a man over the edge in a matter of seconds.

It had taken a little longer with Pierce. She'd been forced to use her tongue, but in the end she felt his body slowly relax, and at the same time come alive.

Five years of playing this game had made her a deadly adversary. Nadja Stefen might have the best hands in the business, but Casmir Balasi had the best set of lips.

A kiss was everything—if it was done right.

Casmir sucked hard on Pierce's lower lip as she broke the kiss, then followed through with one last slow swipe over his lower lip. He had nice lips to go

along with his nice complexion and hard body.
Warm, not dry. Not too thin. Not too full.

Yes, very nice. On a scale of ten, she'd give him
a nine and a half.

When she finished, she looked up at him and
smiled like an expectant bride.

"What's going on?" he muttered. "What are you
up to now?"

"The question is, what are you up to?" She slid
her hand down his chest and ran her hand along the
fly of his jeans.

From the bar the woman broke the moment. "That's
quite a rock, Pierce. I guess congratulations are in
order. When did you decide you were the marrying
kind?"

Casmir turned around to see that all the men
seated at the bar were engaged in the show as well
as the question. Grinning fools, every one of them.

Before Pierce could answer and put his foot between his nice lips, she said, "Life is funny that way.
Love comes when you least expect it." She glanced
back at Pierce. "Isn't that right, honey?" She slipped
her arm around his waist. Playing the giddy bride-
to-be, she laid her hand on his chest. "I love my ring
almost as much as I do the man. It's to die for."

"Now there's a word," he muttered.

She saw his jaw jerk as he glanced down at the
bauble on her finger. She wiggled it, causing the
ring to wink at him. Then she whispered, "You're
supposed to be excited to see me."

He looked at her, faked a smile. "*Oui*, I'm excited.

I can't wait to wring your neck," he whispered back. "Linny, send over a beer. Me and my...bride are going to steal a booth. What are you drinking, *amant?*"

"It's on the bar. I thought I'd try the local favorite and order a beer."

Casmir stepped away from him and sauntered to the bar using a little more hip action than she had when she'd entered the Ginger Root earlier. Beer in hand, she cut across the bar and slipped into the seat across from Pierce in a booth at the back.

The minute she was comfortable, he leaned forward and said, "What the hell do you think you're doing? No one in this town is going to believe I would marry someone like you."

"Someone like me?"

"*Oui,* like you."

"Then I guess you're going to have to work on your acting skills and change their minds. Polax said that I should use my imagination when it came to fitting in with the neighbors. As you said, why would someone *like me* choose a vacation in Le Mystère? And why would I bring my mother along?" Casmir cut him a razor-sharp smile. "I wouldn't. Not unless I wanted Mama to meet the love of my life and soon-to-be husband."

"You're crazy."

"What, so I came for the local color? To enter a beer-guzzling contest? No, let me guess, the summer sack race down main street on Sunday."

He didn't say anything, just scowled.

She went on. "The truth is, the only reason someone *like me* would land in Le Mystère is if I was lost, or kidnapped, or…came to meet the family and friends of the man I love."

Casmir saw the woman behind the bar heading their way with Pierce's beer. "Here's your chance. Convince *Linny* that I'm the one."

"The one?"

"The one you want to spend the rest of your life with. Merrick told Polax you're a man of many talents. Here's your chance to prove it. Serve it up with a smile, honey. The locals are watching."

Thirty minutes later, they walked out of the Ginger Root, Pierce's arm around Casmir's trim waist. He waved to the bar crowd, smiled at Linny, then disappeared out the door with Casmir.

The minute they were out of the bar, he dropped his arm and headed for the Jeep. Suddenly he stopped and held out his hand.

"The key."

Casmir reached into her pocket and tossed it to him, then, ignoring his scowl, climbed into the passenger side of the Jeep. Without another word Pierce climbed behind the wheel. He revved the engine while he stared at her a moment, then spun out of the parking lot kicking up a cloud of dust.

He headed down a dirt road lined with trees as if he were a race-car driver off the pace. As the minutes ticked by, the trees threatened to take over the road, but he never slowed down. It forced Casmir to lean in to avoid being smacked in the face by the foliage.

The farther they went she noticed that water was slowly creeping toward the road like a dirty sponge. The wind had rearranged her hair, and the heat and dust was exfoliating her face. She wouldn't need a facial for a month.

She was hot and sticky, and wondered why anyone would want to drive an open Jeep when a real car with air conditioning was such a staple in this day and age.

"How far does this road go?"

"It goes until it runs out."

"And how far is that?"

"Another mile or so."

"But the water—"

"This is bayou country."

"What does that mean exactly, bayou country?" she asked.

He glanced at her. "It means any time I get good and sick of you I can drown you on a second's notice."

"So," she began, "have you lived in Sweat Hollow long, Pierce?"

"A good share of my life."

"I suppose that explains it."

"Explains what?"

"Your immunity to the heat."

"Where's this going?"

"I'm trying to bury the hatchet. If we could start over. Maybe get past our differences, and understand a little bit about each other, maybe—"

"A good way to start over would be to call Polax and tell him you made a mistake and your…future husband—" he said the word like he was spitting poison "—has everything back under control."

"I'm not going to tell him that. It shouldn't matter to him what our cover is."

. "*Our* cover?"

"Okay, we didn't discuss it collectively, but you weren't anywhere around."

"Because you stole my Jeep and left me on the side of the road."

"And you weren't going to leave me stranded?"

"Make the call."

Casmir hesitated, then pulled her phone from her pocket. "Okay, I'll tell him that everything is back on schedule, and if I do then—"

"Then I'll reconsider feeding you to Charlie."

"Who's Charlie?"

"Lazie's pet alligator. He lives in the swamp out my back door."

Casmir dialed the number, then put the phone to her ear. But before she got one word out, a snake dropped out of a tree hanging over the road and plopped in her lap.

He had ordered her onto the sofa, and had taken off her shoes. He made some comment about her limp. A likely con, Ruza thought. Without her shoes she couldn't run.

She sat stiff and wary. Her knee ached. She'd twisted it trying to make her getaway. She had matching blisters, a bad knee and a vivid memory of Lazie's mouth assaulting hers.

She needed something to calm her nerves. A double martini for starters. She hadn't felt this vulnerable in years.

She was in the middle of nowhere, had been aroused by a lecher, and she had no idea where Cassie was.

Cassie's welfare at the forefront of everything, she said, "You're in trouble, Mr. Lazie. Big trouble. You have no idea who you're dealing with. I'm connected in high places. Places you don't even know exist."

Her threat didn't build a fire under his slow swagger, or change the expression on his confident, craggy face. As if they were now old friends, he knelt down and took her right foot in his hand and examined it.

"I noticed *da* limp. Now I *sees* why. You got a pair of blisters, *mon coeur.*"

She knew what was causing her to limp. Her shoes had rubbed her toes raw.

Ruza watched as his hands slid over her heel and cupped the sole of her foot. The brute had bad manners, and soft hands. She studied his hands. On three of his fingers he wore large silver rings. One in the shape of a crossbones, another sporting a scorpion. Dear Lord, she'd been captured by a modern-day pirate.

He stood and removed his red satin vest and tossed it in a chair.

Now what? If he went for the zipper of his jeans what would she do? She glanced at her shoes. She would need them to make a run for it, provided that her knee cooperated.

He'd removed the keys from his car and they were now in his pocket. It would do her no good to escape the house if she couldn't use the car to get away. She'd be lost within two minutes in the woods.

A city—even a foreign one—she could negotiate. But woods full of trees and animals... No, she'd be prey of another kind.

She glanced around the living room. From the outside it looked like a bare-bones cabin. But on the inside it was cozy and clean. The walls were wood paneling, and the furnishings were old, but in good shape. She saw a wooden rocker, and a stuffed chair that was big enough to curl up in.

She bounced her tush to confirm that the sofa had a good set of springs, then felt a rush of mixed emotions, and at the forefront, panic.

"If you try anything, Lazie, I'll scream and claw you to shreds."

Her warning brought a smile to his face. He stood and walked away.

"Is this your house?" she managed.

From somewhere else, another room, he called out, "It belongs to a friend of mine."

"Does your friend have a name?"

"Pierce Fourtier."

Ruza recognized the name. Her pounding heart slowed. If he was telling the truth, then she wasn't in danger.

"Where is he now?"

"With your daughter. *Der* comin' soon, *cher.*"

Was that the truth? Ruza had learned from experience not to jump ship before there was a rescue boat in sight. If Cassie was on her way, then it would be best to be patient.

When Lazie returned, he was carrying a first-aid kit and a small brown bottle. He knelt again and took her injured feet and propped them on his thigh.

"Women and *dere* crazy shoes." With his index finger—the one sporting the crossbones—he dabbed the smelly liquid on her blisters. Whatever was in the bottle was potent, and the pain immediately lessened. Maybe she should ask if she could rub a little into her knee?

"*Dat's* it, *mon coeur.* A bandage, and you'll be good as new. Now I'll fix us somethin' to eat. There should be a catch of mudbugs in *da* cage under *da* dock. I'll have a look-see."

She was hungry, but her culinary tastes for the unusual only went so far. "I don't eat bugs."

He chuckled. "*Deze* are real tasty bugs. You'll like *dem, cher.*" He grinned, then winked. "I'm a good cook. It's a talent of mine, among other *tings,* Ruza-a…."

She knew what he was referring to. Yes, a rogue was what he was. A pirate with an appetite for more than bugs.

She pulled her foot off his leg. "I also have a few talents, Mr. Lazie. One of them is spotting a silver-tongued devil with nasty business on his mind. I warn you that I'm not as helpless as I look."

Like before her words made him smile, then it turned into a wolf's grin. He stood. "*Oui.* A spirited *ange. Da* most interestin' kind."

When he left the house he was whistling. Ruza tried to stand, and her knee gave out. Her fanny bounced back onto the sofa, confirming the springs were loaded for action. She would give Cassie two hours, and if she didn't show, she was going to put plan B into effect.

She only hoped she would be able to figure out what that was before time ran out.

Her scream damn near put them in the ditch. Pierce slammed on the brakes at the same time as he reached out and snatched the snake from her lap.

With a mighty heave, he slung the reptile out of the Jeep back to where it came from.

"That was a snake!"

"And not a very nice one."

"It was poisonous?"

"Just a bit."

"A bit?"

"Next time, instead of screaming your head off, just get rid of it."

"Get rid of it? You mean touch it?"

"Saying please usually doesn't work when you're talking to a snake. They don't have ears."

She was still breathing heavy, and it was the first time he'd witnessed the vulnerable side of Casmir Balasi. Pierre studied her a long minute, took in her fancy suit and impractical shoes.

"What are you looking at?"

"A woman out of her element."

"Because I'm not fond of snakes?"

"I suppose most women don't like snakes."

"But you, on the other hand, feel right at home in snake heaven."

"I grew up with them. Call Polax."

"First I want some guarantees."

"Like what?"

"While I'm staying at your house we won't invite your cold-blooded neighbors in for a visit?"

"I can't guarantee that. I live in the bayou. Make the call. Tell Polax that my neighbors are growing on you and so am I."

"At least guarantee me that your house has windows, and an indoor bathroom."

"That I can do."

"Can I trust you?"

"*Oui.* I always tell it like it is, *amant.* No bullshit. It's the one thing you can count on."

"And Charlie?"

"Lazie's pet alligator hasn't been in my house since he was five feet long, outgrew the couch and ate the dog."

"He ate the dog?"

The look on her face was priceless. Pierce couldn't keep a straight face. He laughed out loud.

"You jerk."

"Sorry. I couldn't resist."

She made a face at him. Stuck out her tongue.

"By the way, that's a pretty talented tongue."

"Are we burying the hatchet?"

"That's up to you. Call Polax."

"Promise me that Mama is all right and that Lazie hasn't…you know?"

"*Oui.*"

"No bullshit?"

"No bullshit."

Five minutes later Pierce pulled into his driveway, which was crowded with oak trees dressed in Spanish moss, and parked the Jeep next to Lazie's Eldorado. While Casmir made the call to Polax, he got out of the Jeep and stretched his legs. Keeping one ear on the conversation, he stared at the house he'd built years ago. It wasn't much, but at the time he'd built it, it was more than he'd ever had growing up.

He heard her mention the heat to Polax. Today was a comfortable ninety-six in the shade. The cabin wasn't air-conditioned and tomorrow was supposed to be hotter.

Now why did that make him smile?

Chapter 8

Yurii picked up the phone just as he was headed to bed. "What do you know, Nicky?"

"I have her location. She's in Louisiana."

"What do you suppose she's doing there?"

"I'm not sure, but she's with someone. She left town with him in a Jeep and they arrived at a cabin in the woods a short time ago."

"Who is he?"

"His name is Pierce Fourtier."

"Local?"

"He looks like it."

"Not good enough. I'll have Filip check him out. I want to know what his interest is in my *Kisa.*" Yurii lay down on the bed. "Tell me, Nicky, how does my beautiful fiancée look? Describe her to me. Don't leave anything out."

"She looks…well."

"Healthy is good. What else? What was she wearing?"

"A blue pantsuit."

"Fitted?"

"Yes."

"And her hair?"

"Up, like she used to wear it on the yacht. She looked hot. This place is in the middle of a swamp and there are enough bugs here to feed a starving continent for a year. It's damn uncomfortable."

"I don't care about your discomfort, Nicky. You will be well paid."

Yurii closed his eyes and imagined Casmir taking the clip from her hair. Imagined the mass moving around her naked shoulders. Imagined her bending over him on the bed and teasing his cock with her hair like she used to do.

The thought made him hard and hungry for her.

"Before we move forward, I want to know who this man is and what his connection is to my *Kisa*. Sit tight. Watch and wait. Don't disappointment me, Nicky."

"I won't disappoint you, Don Petrov. Never."

"Never is a dangerous word, Nicky. It could get you hung by your heels if you make a mistake. Where is your partner?"

"Anton is watching the cabin."

"Good. Stay put, and keep your eyes open while

Filip runs a check on Fourtier. Contact me in the morning. I should know something by then."

When Yurii hung up he closed his eyes and imagined that *Kisa* was next to him, curled up on her side like she used to do.

He always slept on his back. It was better for his injured foot. But tonight he forced himself to curl his body around the image of *Kisa* in his bed.

That night he slept better than he had in months.

The minute Casmir saw her mother sprawled out on the sofa she turned a glaring eye on the gypsy scum who stood in the doorway of the kitchen.

"If you've harmed a single hair on her head, you're dead, Gypsy."

"Gypsy?"

"You heard me." She eyed the dish towel around his waist, then the spatula in his hand. "Did you... touch my mother?"

"I confess I did. She has blisters on her feet. I put a salve on them."

"That's it?"

"Oui."

Casmir didn't buy it. "I know what you're planning, and I'm here to tell you to forget it."

"I'm planning only dinner for four in a half an hour, *cher.* Ruza-a...how about another martini?"

The question had Casmir glancing at her mother again. She looked like a limp rag. The culprit, two empty glasses on the coffee table.

"I thought I told you to stay put, Mama. I thought I said no martinis."

"Cassie, dear." Ruza glanced at Lazie over the back of the sofa. "You weren't lying."

"Never, *mon coeur.*"

Casmir glared at the gypsy.

Pierce said, "We're burying the hatchet, remember? Your mother's fine. What's for dinner, Lazie?"

"Mudbugs."

Casmir was sure she hadn't heard right. The gypsy intended to serve them bugs? The repulsion must have shown on her face.

"Lazie assures me that they're tasty, Cassie," Ruza said. "I don't believe we've been properly introduced, Mr. Fourtier. You're Cassie's coworker?"

"*Oui.* We work for separate…companies, but we have mutual interests."

"Interesting."

Cassie noticed the way her mother gave Pierce a smile of approval after looking him up, then down. "Mama…" She shook her head. "How many martinis have you had?"

"I'm not sure."

Casmir turned to Pierce, gave him a nasty look, then offered one to Lazie. "I believe I'll pass on dinner and opt for a shower and a nap. About our luggage. I left it in the—"

"It's been recovered," Lazie said. "I have it in the Eldorado."

At least the man had one brain cell, Casmir thought. She glanced around the house, seeing it for the first time. It was clean, and there were no snakes curled up in any of the chairs. The windows were made of real glass, and the roof looked solid. One point for Pierce.

"The bathroom," she said. "Which way?"

"Down the hall to your right," Pierce said. "You can take my bedroom. It's across the hall. Your mother can have the one Lazie uses when he's here. He'll bunk out back with me in the screened-in porch."

Casmir headed for the hall. If the bathroom had a door on it and hot running water she'd give Pierce another point. If the bedroom had a mattress off the floor, she'd scratch another point on his bedpost. If not, she was going to call Polax back and chew him a new earhole.

After a long shower, Casmir laid down on the bed in Pierce's room—yes, it had a mattress off the floor—and listened to her mother's laughter. What on earth could be so funny about eating bugs in the company of that long-haired gypsy? she wondered.

Either Mama was sipping another martini, or the gypsy had spiked the bugs.

It was while she began to doze off that she was awakened by a noise outside. She sat up and listened. It sounded like voices. No, it sounded more like someone groaning.

She came to her feet and pulled out her Makarov. She walked to the window, and carefully opened it. When she heard another groan, she returned to the

bed and doused the light on the nightstand. She
slipped on her sexy shoes, wishing she had something more suitable. But Lazie hadn't brought in her
luggage yet.

With her gun in hand, she climbed out the
window into the hot, humid air. Staying close to the
house, she listened again. Polax had sounded a bit
strange on the phone when she'd called him, and she
couldn't forget the last words he'd said to her.

*Stay put. Yurii's about to take the bait. Once he's
bitten you're halfway home.*

Something slid over her foot. Oh, God. If that was
a snake, she was going to scream. What had Polax
been thinking, sending her and Mama out here in the
middle of a swamp? It just didn't make sense.

Another groan—this one closer—had her sucking
close to a tree. Who was out here? She wished she
had alerted Pierce to the fact that something was
amiss before she'd left the cabin.

She heard the sound of a car start up somewhere
in the distance. Pierce's Jeep was still parked out
front. As was Lazie's car.

She stepped on a twig and it snapped loudly. She
silently swore, then kicked off her shoes and left
them, hoping they would still be there when she
returned. She ventured deeper into the woods,
creeping softly. She again refused to think about the
reptile population, or their nightly habits.

She raised her Makarov, stopped and listened.
Nothing.

She decided to return to the cabin and inform

Pierce of what she'd heard. She started back, but she never made it. In a blink of an eye she was tackled. Before she landed, her instincts went into play and she kneed her assailant and elbowed him in the ribs.

She lost the Makarov, and she opened her mouth to scream, but before she could make a noise, a hand covered her mouth. She fought hard. Scratched and clawed.

"Stop it, Cass. It's me, dammit."

He removed his hand and she stopped fighting. Squinted in the darkness to make out Pierce's face. "What are you doing?"

"That's a good question. What are *you* doing?"

"I heard something."

"That's not unusual. This is a bayou, after all."

"I heard groaning and it didn't sound like an animal." Casmir pushed on Pierce's shoulder. "Let me up."

He rolled off her and came to his feet. Offered her a hand up. "You probably heard Charlie."

"And I suppose Charlie can drive? I heard a car."

He didn't let go of her hand. Pulling her along behind him, he said, "Let's go back inside."

"I lost my gun." She pulled away from him, and that was when something stabbed her in the foot. "Ouch."

"What's wrong now?"

"I stepped on something."

He produced a flashlight from his back pocket and directed the beam of light down to her feet. "Where the hell are your shoes?"

"Somewhere between here and your bedroom window. I took them off so I could move more quietly."

"Out here you never go anywhere without shoes."

"Do you remember what my shoes look like? They're not exactly designed to take a hike through the woods in the middle of the night."

"And whose fault is that?"

"Are we fighting again?"

Without warning, he lifted her off her feet and started to carry her back to the cabin.

"Put me down. I need to find my gun."

"Forget it."

"You're so damn stubborn."

He stopped and looked at her. "And you're not?"

"I'm determined. There's a difference. Stubborn is defined as willful and inflexible. Determined means firm and steady."

"Whatever."

"I rest my case. A determined woman would never use the word *whatever.* But a stubborn man who had just been bested by a woman would dismiss the conversation as quickly as possible."

He started walking again.

"Not through the front door. Mama will ask a dozen questions. And don't mention Charlie. She won't sleep a wink if she finds out that you've trained the reptiles to drive."

"Cute."

"So you have noticed."

"Has anyone threatened to sew your mouth shut?"

"I'm calling Polax in the morning and demanding he send us someplace else."

"I thought you said you were determined. A determined woman stands firm, remember?" He pinched her ass. "Not bad. Now if you could just learn to keep your mouth shut."

"My mouth is what has kept me alive for five years. Most men love my mouth."

"So you talk a man to death, is that it?"

"No. I kiss him to death."

"No wonder Polax asked for our help on this mission."

"There's that word again. I wouldn't exactly call this a mission. Not unless you know something I don't. Do you?"

They had reached the bedroom window. He aimed her legs at the open window and thrust her inside. "You missed supper?"

"The menu was bugs," she reminded him, popping her head back out the open window. "I guess that's another difference between us. Taste matters. What about my shoes and my gun?"

"You can look for them in the morning."

"By morning there will be nothing left of my shoes. They're expensive."

"So is my time."

She scowled at him. "If one of your groaning neighbors eats my shoes I'm going to—"

"Don't go out again."

"About my luggage…"

"What about it?"

"I have nothing to wear to bed."

"You should be used to that. Isn't that part of the package when you're kissing a man to death?"

Before she could answer he stepped back and disappeared into the darkness.

"Pierce?"

No answer.

"Pierce."

Casmir swore, then turned around to find her mother sitting on the bed.

"Hi, Mama. How long have you been sitting there?"

"What's going on, Cassie?"

"I...was just talking to Pierce."

"Usually the door is the best way to get outside."

Caught, Casmir decided the truth would be best. "I thought I heard something."

"So you went out the window to see what it was?"

"I know that sounds strange."

"Where are your shoes?"

"I...took them off. You look tired, Mama. It's been a long day. You should get some sleep."

"Why do you suppose Mr. Lazie brought me to the cabin in the trunk of his car?"

"In the trunk?"

"He said you told him to do that."

"You must have misunderstood."

"No, I don't think so. I heard every word."

"Are you sure? You know how you get when you drink, Mama."

"I didn't imagine being kidnapped and tossed in the trunk. What's going on, Cassie?"

"I don't know why Lazie put you in the trunk, Mama, but I'll talk to Pierce about it. Come on now." Casmir held out her hand to her mother. "Let's get you to bed."

Ruza yawned, then got to her feet. "Did you find out what the noise was?"

"Just an animal. That's why you need to stay inside. Promise me."

Ruza patted Casmir's hand as they strolled down the hall. "Of course, dear. You go to bed, too. I'll see you in the morning."

Pierce dropped Casmir's shoes beside the sofa, then went to find Lazie. He was in the kitchen, alone. Ruza Balasi must have gone to bed.

Lazie turned from the sink with soap suds clinging to his hands. "You catch *dem?*"

"*Oui.* One. He's tied to the old oak tree fifty yards from the back door. I want you to take him into New Orleans and lock him up at the Glitterbug. I'll call Merrick and have him send someone to pick him up."

"You *don tink* much of *dis* plan, do you?"

"No plan is ever perfect, but this one stinks."

"*Da* Balasi women are a handful, *dat's* a sure *ting.*"

Pierce couldn't argue with that. "Cass is asking questions. She isn't buying why she's here. I don't like keeping her in the dark like this. Too dangerous."

"*Den* don't. Tell her *da* truth."

"Merrick won't go for that."

"Change his mind. You were always good at *dat*. Running a good argument."

"Petrov knows where she is now. In a few days he'll make his move."

"You want me to set up a little welcome for him?"

"*Oui*. I don't want it to be too easy for him to take her from me. That could make him suspicious. So feel free to use your imagination."

Lazie grinned. "It'll be a pleasure, *mon ami*. It's been years since I've had a chance to go a little crazy."

"When you get to the Glitterbug and settle our friend, hire Frog to guard him overnight. Tell him there's a grand in it if he wants to play."

"He'll play for less."

"But he's worth a grand. Tell him I said so."

Lazie dried his hands, and untied the dishcloth from around his waist. "I'll take off right away."

"Remember, these guys enjoy playing rough. Watch your back."

"And you watch *da* ladies. I want *ta* learn more about Cookie. She's *da* kind of woman a man meets once in a lifetime."

Pierce didn't comment, though he wasn't sure when Lazie learned the story behind the famous stage actress he would like any of it.

This mission was a can of worms, as his friend Bjorn Odell would say. He didn't like the way Merrick and Polax had chosen to keep Casmir in the dark. Maybe Lazie was right. Maybe when he called Merrick about the two men spying on them in the woods, he'd express his feelings. She should know the game and how she was supposed to play her hand. And there was also the possibility that she could take off with her mother before the game started.

"You said you picked up their luggage?"

"It's in *da* car. I'll toss it out before I take our friend for a ride."

After Lazie left, Pierce called Merrick. He told him that Petrov knew their location, and that he'd apprehended one of Yurii's spies. He told Merrick he could pick up the man at the Glitterbug in New Orleans in the morning. He also told him that he wanted to share the mission information with Casmir.

Merrick didn't agree that it was necessary, but Pierce turned stubborn in his argument, and in the end Merrick conceded.

"All right, I'm giving you clearance to tell her just enough to keep her butt grounded in Le Mystère until Petrov makes his move. Lev won't be happy about it, but I'll tell him what you said. We can't afford for her to take off. Balasi is this mission. Without her we have nothing."

"Exactly."

Pierce hung up, then picked up the luggage off the porch where Lazie had left it before he'd rounded up their hostage and headed for town. He stepped back inside and set Ruza's bag down behind the couch, then hooked a finger through the straps on Casmir's sexy blue shoes.

He grabbed her travel bag, and had just started down the hall when he saw her dart out of the bathroom and into the bedroom wearing nothing but a towel.

Chapter 9

When Casmir spied Pierce in the hall she didn't say anything; she breezed into the bedroom never expecting that he would follow her. Her hand was on the door when he pushed his way inside.

"Why don't you come in?"

"I thought you'd never ask." He handed her shoes to her, then dropped her bag on the bed next to her clothes.

"A nice gesture. My gun?"

He pulled it from his pocket and laid it on the nightstand. "We need to talk."

She noticed his jaw was set. He was here to tell her something she wasn't going to like.

She closed the door, then bent to set her shoes on the floor.

"Another shower?"

When she straightened, she caught him eyeing her thighs. "My feet were dirty. Do you have a robe I could use?"

"Never owned one."

"That doesn't surprise me."

"Shy in front of your fiancé."

"Very funny."

She rounded the bed and unzipped her bag. Much to her disappointment, she saw that she was going to have to live without a robe, and a lot more than that. Whoever had packed for her obviously didn't know where she was going, or how long she was staying. There were three outfits inside—none of them appropriate for the swamp. Ditto on both pairs of shoes.

When she looked up, Pierce had grabbed her teal blue bra from the bed.

"Interesting color."

If he got a thrill fondling her bra, let him. If he was trying to intimidate her, let him try.

Casmir went to sit in the wicker chair in the corner of the room. She settled her butt down and tucked the towel firmly into place above her breasts. As she relaxed and crossed her legs, she noticed Pierce's eyes zeroing in on the edge of the towel. Any second now he would begin to picture what he couldn't see.

She raised her hand and ran her fingers through

her hair, spreading the wet strands over her shoulders. "You wanted to talk."

"I didn't come to play one of your games."

"Then maybe you should put my bra back where you found it."

"Territorial? That wasn't in your file."

"Neither was your fetish for lingerie."

He smiled, then tossed her bra back on the bed and walked to the window. He pulled the curtains together, and when he turned to face her he was no longer smiling.

"Since I was recruited this morning I haven't agreed with the agenda for this mission. When an agent steps into a snake's den you don't go in with your eyes closed."

"Are we on a mission, Pierce? I was told I was on vacation."

"*Oui,* we're on a mission."

"Are you here to open my eyes and tell me what kind of snake den has brought us together?"

"*Oui.* The why of it, at least. I told Merrick a little while ago that I don't care how good the reason is—deaf and dumb, in my book, gets you dead."

"In this case I'm the deaf and dumb one, right?"

He relaxed against the wall next to the window and crossed his arms over his chest. Casmir didn't like the direction this conversation was going. She had been suspicious from the beginning, and now Pierce had just confirmed that Polax had conned her in some way. He would only do that if he knew she wasn't going to like the outcome.

Needing to keep the ill feelings at bay, she went into survival mode. She was beginning to feel like a cat with one paw in a trap and the other three in quicksand.

"You know, Pierce, I never liked you in Austria. You thought I was a dumb blonde then, too. I assure you I'm not as dumb as you think. And I never go anywhere with my eyes closed."

"I don't think you're dumb, *amant*. What you are is loyal, and that's what Polax was counting on when he cooked up this subterfuge with Merrick."

"Meaning?"

"Meaning he didn't have to spill his guts to make you pack your bags."

"They were already packed."

"*Oui*, there you go. He was damn sure of you. So sure, he mapped out this mission knowing you would go wherever he sent you."

"And are you going to spill your guts and tell me why I'm here? At the same time maybe you could explain why Lazie kidnapped my mother and brought her here in his trunk?"

"Today didn't go as planned. You took off and—"

"You didn't show up when and where you were supposed to."

"Okay, so I should have met you."

"What was that? You're admitting you made the mistake?"

"If it makes you feel better."

"It does."

"At the Glitterbug I told Lazie to get Ruza out of there and bring her here. My guess is he felt she wasn't going to cooperate, so he made a decision."

"One I'm having difficulty explaining to her."

"That can't be changed now. Let's talk about Yurii Petrov."

Casmir's body tensed. "Let's not."

"I know what happened between you two. I read the report."

If he had read the report, he didn't know the half of it.

"If you have the details then you talk and I'll listen."

"I got clearance from Merrick to summarize the mission's agenda. Like I said, Polax should have been up-front with you."

"Spill your guts. I'm all ears."

"You're the bait."

She'd heard that word before. Polax had used it in Prague, and on the phone when they'd last talked.

"I'm the bait?" A knot gripped Casmir's stomach. She now understood. "I'm here to lay a trap for Yurii? He attempts to kill me and you recapture him in the process, is that it?"

"Not exactly. Simply returning him to prison isn't enough to crush his operation."

"I'd say they learned that a little late. I spent four months in his—"

"Bed." His eyes stared her down.

"I did my job."

"*Oui*. Quite well. I heard you had Petrov eating out of your hand."

"No, it was actually one of my shoes."

"He asked you to marry him."

To that, Casmir made no comment. She had done what was necessary to complete the mission. All anyone needed to know—including Polax, and now Pierce—was relevant facts.

He continued to stare her down.

It was the eyes of judgment, at least that was what it felt like. And it pissed her off. "You're a real tough guy, Pierce. You play with guns and knives, move in quick and get out quicker. If you feel like screwing it's on your own time and you don't have to fill out a report afterward. Well, screwing is my job, tough guy, not my hobby. I did my job, and filled out a report. It's not my fault it didn't solve all Quest's problems with Yurii Petrov. Maybe they should have had a backup plan."

"No argument here."

"You said I'm the bait. Obviously Quest thinks Yurii will come after me, or at least send someone to kill me. What am I missing?"

"His headquarters is believed to be in the Mediterranean, but no one knows where. He keeps an extensive database on past and current clients, as well as his own diverse business information. While you were taking Yurii down months ago, I was coming off a mission in Greece. You've heard of the Chameleon?"

"Yes. Onyxx's nemesis who refuses to die."

"Petrov launders the Chameleon's money. That connection is Onyxx's interest in this. As Merrick told me, when agencies work together, good things happen."

Casmir stood. She had never expected to see Yurii again after she had sent him to prison. Had prayed she would never have to face him again. Then four days ago he'd shown up in Bratislava, and all those days and nights with him had come flooding back.

Be careful when tempting the devil. Especially when you've stolen his soul.

Pierce was still talking. She stopped pacing and faced him, suddenly realizing the game. "You want me to lead you to Yurii's hideout."

"That's right. He takes the bait, and we follow once you've been captured."

The perfect bait. The perfect worm on the hook.

"What if he simply wants me dead?"

"You don't believe that, do you?"

She didn't know what to believe right now. "I suppose you've figured out a way to let him know where to find me."

"He already knows where you are. Tonight the noise you heard was me. Two men have been watching the cabin since the moment we arrived. I let one get away. We don't want this to look too easy."

"You think he'll take me to Nescosto Priyatna."

"*Oui.*"

"And if he doesn't?"

"Right now Yurii's a wanted man. His hideout is the safest place for him. We think he'll send someone after you, with instructions to bring you to him."

"Polax should have told me."

"I agree."

If he had, then maybe she would have found a way to share with him the reasons why this mission wasn't going to work out the way they had planned.

She turned away. Pierce was right; her loyalty to Quest had kept her in Polax's pocket. He'd sat in his big chair and lied to her. He'd set her up and pretended to be concerned about her safety. And what about Mama? How dare he risk her life!

You're in the deep freeze until we can find another use for you.

Well he had certainly found a use for her. The term *bait* wasn't the right one, however. She was their sacrificial lamb.

"Once you're in, and we have the location, I'll retrieve the data, and pick you up on the way out."

What an arrogant ass. Casmir turned to face him. "If you think it will be that easy, you're even a bigger fool than Polax. If you're lucky enough to get out, I suggest you leave my body there. It will slow you down on your escape."

"Have a little faith, *amant*."

"I never go into a job riding on the wings of faith, Pierce. If I did, I wouldn't have survived my first mission. I know the intelligence world places little value on women operatives. I've heard the jokes, and the comments. Most agencies consider us expendable. I just didn't know Polax felt the same way. I guess prostitution in any form is legal when your pimp is the government."

"As I said, you should have been told up front, but

that's something you'll have to take up with Polax when we get back."

Casmir crossed the room and pulled her phone from her jacket pocket, but before she could use it, Pierce stripped it out of her hand.

"Calling him isn't going to change anything. Petrov already knows where you are. The game has started."

"Give me my phone."

"No."

"Give me my phone."

When she grabbed for it, he reached out and pulled her against him. She fought him, shoved hard, and that was when the towel went to the floor. Before she could rescue it, she was on the bed, Pierce flattening her out on her back.

"Listen to me."

"Get off."

"I don't like this any better than you do, but it is what it is. Trust me. I'll get you out of this alive."

She looked away, so angry that she felt like crying. That wouldn't do. She didn't cry in front of men.

"You're hurting me."

"Look at me."

"Just get off and get out."

"I want your promise that you'll do this. Merrick warned me that if I told you you might turn chickenshit. Prove him wrong. Prove them all wrong. And when this is over—"

She looked at him, willing strength back in her voice. "And when this is over you'll send flowers to my funeral. Agreed?"

"There isn't going to be any damn funeral."

"I'm partial to orchids. And don't be stingy. A dozen is a nice gesture, but two is always more impressive. At least I deserve that much."

"I won't let you die."

"Orchids. Two dozen. Promise me."

"Sonofabitch."

"Promise me."

"All right. Orchids. Two fucking dozen."

"When you ride to my rescue, remember to bring along a body bag to pick up the pieces. Yurii isn't going to let me go home beautiful."

He swore again, then climbed off her. Naked, feeling his eyes on her, she curled into a ball on her side. Seconds later she felt the towel that had dropped to the floor cover her.

"I'm leaving the phone. Don't call Polax. Trust me instead, *amant*."

Pierce had smoked close to a pack of cigarettes by the time Lazie got back from New Orleans. He stood on the porch leaning against a newel post as his friend got out of the Eldorado.

Once Lazie climbed the steps, he said, "I got our friend settled."

"Did Frog agree to guard him?"

"He was happy to do it. He told me *ta* tell you, whatever you need, just give him a call."

"Good."

"Been *tinkin' dis* situation over. When you gonna tell me all of it?"

"I figure now is as good a time as any to tell you how you figure into this."

"Am I going to like it?"

Pierce lit a cigarette.

"I'll take one of *dem.*"

"Thought you quit."

"I did. Now I'm what you call a social smoker. I only light up when I'm socializin'."

"You socialize at the Glitterbug every day."

Lazie grinned. "*Dat* I do. But now I *don* hear the criticism. Folks *tink* I'm smokin' with *dem* to be nice. Sacrificin' for *dem.* Makes *dem* feel special, and I *don* hear any lectures on health issues."

Pierce smiled. "You're crazy, Lazie."

"So tell me what I should know. What's got you upset?"

"How do you know I'm upset?"

"It's a fact you *don* show it much. But I know you better *den* most. *Da* way your puffin' and grippin' *dat* life saver says it all. You have words with *une belle femme?*"

"A few."

"It didn't go well?"

"Horseshit. She hated me before. Now we've turned the corner and headed down an even blacker alley."

"*Dat don* sound like you. You always could charm *da* pants off of a *fille* no matter how tight *da* fit."

"This is a squeeze all right."

"A nice word, squeeze. It reminds me of what's sleepin' in my bed. So what do you want from me?"

"Your promise that you won't let Ruza Balasi out of your sight for the next couple of days. How do you feel about being her bodyguard?"

Lazie grinned, then blew smoke. "I *tink* I'm goin' *ta* like *dis* job just fine."

Yurii was on his way to meet the Chameleon when he called Nicky. He was on his yacht, the *Bella Vella,* just leaving the Gulf of Salerno.

"Pierce Fourtier works for Onyxx? He's a level-one agent, Filip tells me. So I've been asking myself, why would Onyxx involve themselves with an agent from Quest? What's in it for them?"

"And have you come up with an answer, Don Petrov?"

"Not yet. But I will."

"Your news explains what just happened."

"And what has happened, Nicky?"

"I have some bad news. Fourtier surprised us while we were staking out his cabin. I don't know how he knew we were there, but... I was careful. Only—"

"Only what, Nicky?"

"Anton was captured."

"You disappoint me, Nicky. And in the past week I've had too many disappointments."

"I need another man."

"It sounds like you need more than one. Filip told me that Fourtier is one of Onyxx's best."

"I'm sorry, Don Petrov."

"I want *Kisa* back, Nicky. No excuses. I will send someone to take over the capture."

"But— Whatever you say, Don Petrov."

"In four days, Nicky. I want *Kisa* at Nescosto Priyatna in four days."

"She will be there."

Yurii didn't like the idea of Onyxx entering the game. What puzzled him was why they would be interested in *Kisa*. Or was he looking at this all wrong? Maybe *Kisa* wasn't the interest. Maybe it was him.

He rubbed his jaw, considered the idea.

He said, "Do not fail me again, Nicky. If you do, I will cut your heart out and eat it myself."

"Yes, Don Petrov. When will you send the men?"

"You will have them tonight. Give me a location where they can meet you."

"I'm in Le Mystère. The men can find me at a bar called the Ginger Root. I'll be there all night waiting for them."

"One more thing, Nicky. After you have sent *Kisa* on her way to me, stay behind and kill Pierce Fourtier. Make sure he suffers."

Yurii pocketed his phone after making a second call. He sent Nicky five men. Five bloodthirsty Russian *soldatos* who were eager to please him, and one unexpected surprise.

Standing on the deck of his yacht, he again felt anxious to get his business with the Chameleon settled so he could focus his attention on the proper welcome-home gift for *Kisa*.

A woman with so much beauty should never sell herself so cheaply. Quest was about to learn a lesson they would not soon forget. They were about to lose one of their best and most talented to the enemy.

"Until death do us part," Yurii whispered. "*Da*, until death, *Kisa*."

Chapter 10

Casmir slept in later than she'd planned. She hadn't been able to fall asleep until close to morning. She climbed out of bed tired and irritable. Already hot.

She sorted through the items in her bag. It wouldn't take long to figure out what to wear today. She had two choices—a sexy uneven-hemmed pink floral skirt and blouse, or a black silk shift. Both outfits had matching lingerie and sandals.

She hadn't called Polax after Pierce had left the bedroom. She had wanted to—still wanted to—but she was too angry to speak to him yet. And when she did, she wanted to know everything. She suspected Pierce was holding something back. He hadn't mentioned why her mother had been sent along. Polax might be planning to sacrifice her for the sake of Quest, but Mama, too?

She believed that Pierce knew the answer to that question, and she intended to get it out of him one way or another. If she was going to be dangled in front of Yurii like a piece of meat, so be it. But not Mama.

She pulled out the pink underwear, grabbed the skirt and blouse, and pink shoes. Fifteen minutes later she walked out of the bathroom, showered and dressed, to check on Mama. Not finding her in her bedroom, she entered the living room, then the kitchen.

When she discovered no one was in the house, she stepped out on the porch to find Pierce leaning against a post, smoking. That was no surprise.

"Where's Mama?"

"Lazie took her for a boat ride."

"A boat ride? Where?"

"To tour the bayou, then to lunch at a little place on the river."

"And you let her go?"

"She seemed eager."

"I doubt that. You forced her to go with him, didn't you?"

"I wouldn't use the word *force*. I didn't put a gun to her head, or threaten to put her back in the trunk."

"Cute. Call Lazie and tell him to bring her back."

"No."

Casmir swore. "I don't trust him. Every time he looks at Mama he starts to drool."

He continued to smoke and look out over the murky water. "I think she likes him."

"About as much as she likes sour milk."

"Lazie's a nice guy."

"He's a randy dog."

"That, too."

Finally he turned to look at her standing in the doorway. "It seems the stories are true."

"What stories?"

He looked her up and down. "That the actress never has a hair out of place."

"Is that some kind of offhanded compliment? If you think flattery is going to score points, you're wasting your time."

"Did you call Polax?"

"Not yet. I know that what you told me last night barely scratched the surface. This morning I want to know the rest of it."

"The rest?"

"Why was my mother sent with me? If I'm going to be a sitting duck, fine, but I will not allow my mother to be placed in danger."

"She's going to be fine. Want breakfast?"

"No. What I want is my mother out of harm's way."

"Done."

"Just like that?"

"Just like that."

"I don't believe you."

"I'm hungry. Do you cook?"

"I can cook when I want to. I rarely want to."

He walked past her into the house and headed for the kitchen.

She trailed him. "If the roles were reversed would you be willing to put your life in my hands? The life of your mother?"

He opened the fridge. "I don't have a mother."

"Everyone has a mother."

He took out a carton of orange juice. "Want some?"

"No."

He popped it open and drained the carton, then tossed it into the sink.

"You're avoiding the question. You probably don't even know who your mother is."

"I know. She gave me life, but we never bonded. Not like you and Ruza. You can trust that if you do what I tell you your mother will be out of here before the action starts."

"That's not good enough."

"Maybe if we spend some quality time together you'll get more comfortable with the word *trust*... and me." He gave her another head-to-toe. "I wonder what you'd look like in a pair of jeans."

"If you read my file you already know that I can fit into any mold required of me. In Austria, I—"

"Wore ass-tight black pants and a blue sweater. *Oui,* I remember the day we met."

"I remember you, too. Whining after you got shot."

He glanced down to her feet. "Pink sandals. Don't you own a pair of decent shoes?"

"My shoes aren't important at the moment. What is, is that Mama is taken someplace safe, and Polax pays for being a lying bastard. I intend to haunt him from the grave."

"You're a woman who holds grudges, then?"

"Something to remember."

"I'll keep it in mind."

She had decided just before she'd fallen asleep last night that she would go through with the mission. For a split second she had considered running away, but she was no coward. And because she wasn't, that left her only one choice—play Polax's game, and in the end, Yurii's.

It was crazy thinking, but she wished that Pierce had some superpower she didn't know about. That he would be able to pull a miracle out of his nice, tight ass pocket and make good on his promise. She would have liked to trust him, but how could she trust an agent who smoked too much, and probably couldn't sprint a hundred yards without his lungs collapsing?

"What are you thinking?"

"Nothing."

"It must be something. You're not usually this quiet."

She shrugged off his little dig, sat down at the table. It would do no good to share her little secrets now. As he had said, the mission had started, and Yurii knew where to find her. It was only a matter of time now.

He fixed scrambled eggs and toast for the both of them. While they ate, he said, "I need to make a grocery run. Unless you're interested in trying out mudbugs?"

Casmir sat back and wiped her mouth on her napkin. "I think it would be a good idea if you ran along into town. I'll stay here and wait for Mama."

"I'd rather you go with."

"Afraid Yurii's going to kidnap me while you're gone?"

"His men won't come until tomorrow."

"How do you know that?" She held up her hand. "Forget the question. I'm sure that's privileged information. The bait doesn't need to know when, just be available."

"I understand how you feel."

"You don't know shit about how I feel, so don't patronize me." She picked up her empty plate and carried it to the sink.

"Polax wouldn't have put you in this situation if he didn't think you could handle it and come out alive."

"Well, he doesn't know everything," Casmir muttered to herself.

"What did you say?"

"Nothing."

"Do you know something we don't? Something you left out of your report?"

She turned from the sink. "It doesn't matter now. As you said, it's started."

"If it makes a difference it matters."

"In my five years at Quest I've never been conned by my own agency. At the moment I'm not feeling too loyal, or too generous with anything I left out of that report."

"Then you did leave something out. What?"

"It won't ruin your record, Agent Pierce. I'm sure you'll succeed in getting your data. You're a tough guy." Casmir mocked him by flexing her muscles.

"I'll get you out."

"Maybe I'd just as soon you didn't."

Suddenly he was on his feet. "What the hell does that mean?"

She started past him and he grabbed her arm. "Explain that last comment."

She jerked free. "If I survive this, it will be my decision, and I'll save myself. When the time comes, get the data and get out."

She headed into the living room.

Pierce called after her. "I'm leaving in thirty minutes for Le Mystère. Be ready."

"Whatever you say, Agent Fourtier."

"And when we get into town, remember, we're a happy couple, so sharpen up those acting skills... *amant*. Today you're in love, and I'm the lucky man."

Love... Casmir glanced down at the ring on her finger. Sometimes love could be the death of you.

Ruza sat in Lazie's boat and watched him maneuver them through the bayou. It was far more beautiful here than she'd expected. The crazy thing was she had agreed to leave Cassie asleep at the cabin and go out on the water with the very man who had tossed her into a trunk.

She eyed the man. Today Lazie had left his garish vest and frilly shirt at home. He wore a black T-shirt and jeans. His body looked younger than his suspected age. She understood now why he had been able to wrestle her to the ground yesterday.

The man had muscular arms, and the agility of a man in his thirties, not his late fifties. But then, age was experience, and this man looked as if he'd lived his life to the fullest.

He had given her a brief history of the area, named every tree they passed, and where every water trail went. The information had her head spinning. Or was it Lazie himself that was spinning her head?

She had never in all her travels met anyone like him. He was rough around the edges, and spoke a language all his own.

"I've been waiting to hear why you accosted me yesterday, Mr. Lazie."

He turned to look at her. "Is *dat* why you said *oui* to *dis* boat ride, Cookie?"

"I guess it is."

"*Non.* I *don tink* so."

"What do you think my reason was, then?"

He grinned. "I *tink* you like me."

"And why would I like a man who tossed me in a trunk?"

"I'm sorry about *dat.* In a day or two, maybe three, you'll understand, but for now, I *tink* let's just enjoy each other. Are you gettin' hungry yet, Cookie? Bubba's Place is a few miles up and around *da* bend."

"Bubba's?"

"Bubba's got *de* best rib shack on *da* river."

"A restaurant?"

"You could call it *dat.* It started out as a fishin' shack. *Den* the word got out *dat* Bubba could cook like his mama. Been cookin' for *da* folks around here ever since."

She would be hungry soon. She'd only had a piece of toast for breakfast after she'd seen what Lazie was having—leftover mudbugs from the night before.

"Ribs, you said?"

"Barbecued ribs and hush puppies. Bubba's are *da* best I ever ate."

Ruza wasn't sure if that was a good selling point. Lazie's taste in food was questionable. She had given the mudbugs a try last night, and they hadn't tasted too bad. The problem was touching them. And there was no way she could put the head of the thing in her mouth to suck the juice, as Lazie had showed her how to do.

"So, Cookie, should we stop?"

She needed to use a bathroom. "All right, Lazie, we'll eat at the restaurant, but only if you promise I won't be disappointed, there's a bathroom, and I won't be accosted by the natives."

Her last comment drew a smile. He said, "If any man lays a hand on you, *mon coeur,* I'll cut him in half."

"It's comforting to know you're watching my back, Lazie."

He patted the wicked knife strapped on his belt that was too big to fit in his pocket. "A comfort for you, and my pleasure."

In a strange way Lazie reminded her of Jacko. Not in appearance or dress, but they were both take-charge men. Maybe that was the attraction. Cassie's father had had a wild side, too. He'd been exciting and handsome. Lazie could be wickedly handsome in his own way.

She wondered what he would look like with his hair cut, a shave and new clothes.

She caught Lazie staring, his devil eyes moving slowly over her breasts and legs. He was thinking nasty thoughts again. She set aside the picture in her mind of him clean shaven. It would take more than a few surface improvements to make him fit into her world.

They rounded the bend and that was when the rib shack came into sight. Ruza wasn't surprised by its size. Lazie had said it was small. What surprised her was how many boats were tied up to the floating dock.

Bubba's ribs must be edible, she thought.

When Lazie tied up the boat, he helped her climb out. Once on the dock, he let her go ahead of him. She knew why, knew his eyes had drifted to her backside.

She said over her shoulder, "That's not what I meant when I said watch my back."

He chuckled. "*Mais* yeah, a spirited *ange. Da* best kind, my Ruza-a…."

Merrick went to visit Sarah Finny at the flower shop and to pick up the two dozen roses for Johanna. He spoke to Sarah kindly, and even found himself flirting with her. She smiled, and that was when he asked her to dinner.

He and Sarah had been steadily getting closer, but he hadn't kissed her yet. Maybe tomorrow after dinner he would take the next step. He liked her company, liked how easy she was to be around.

A woman's voice, her laughter... Yes, he'd missed both. Johanna had loved to laugh.

He left the flower shop with the roses and drove to the cemetery north of the city. As he walked to Johanna's grave, he began to feel guilty. He'd just arranged a date with Sarah, and now he was planning to spend the afternoon with Johanna.

He couldn't stop seeing Johanna, and yet he ached for a real life. For a woman to touch, and to be touched.

Would Johanna understand? She had been a jealous woman when they were together, but not nearly as jealous as he had been. If a man looked at her twice he had wanted to take his head off.

So what was he doing? Sarah deserved a man who could love her with his whole heart, and that would never be him.

At Johanna's grave, Merrick placed the roses in the silver vase, then went to sit on the bench.

"It's sunny today, Johanna. The sky's clear and the air summer warm. Do you remember what day it is? Today is your birthday. You're forty-one. Remember what we always did on your birthday? Dinner at LuCasa and a movie. It never mattered what movie. Then afterward..."

Merrick closed his eyes as the vision of the two of them took shape by the fire in the home they had shared. They would talk of their dreams for a family, of growing old together. Then make love.

He could feel her now touching him. Feel her shiver as he entered her. The fever would always take them quickly, each time as fresh and new as the first.

Merrick stayed two hours with Johanna, and as he walked back to his car, he called Sarah and canceled their dinner for tomorrow night. It was as he was on his way back to the city that Polax called.

"I didn't expect to hear from you so soon. Is something wrong?"

"You bet your ass something's wrong. Your agent told Casmir she's the bait."

Merrick remained calm. "Did she call you?"

"No. I called her to check on how things were going."

"And she took your head off for lying to her."

"No. She was as cold as a fish. Then she said something that waved a red flag."

"And that was…?"

"She told me she wanted Ruza out of Le Mystère immediately, and that if something happened to her, she wanted me to promise that Ruza would be taken care of. She demanded that I put it in writing. She knows our plan. Dammit, Adolf, your agent had no right to—"

"I gave him clearance to tell her. Not everything, just enough to keep her at the cabin. Pierce thought it would be best if—"

"I know what's best for Casmir. I need her a hundred percent when Petrov gets his hands on her. He's ruthless, and if he senses this is a setup, he could kill her before we can get her out of there."

"Pierce is a damn good agent. If I didn't trust him to do the job, I wouldn't have supported this mission. Maybe you should call Balasi back and tell her everything. I mean everything, Lev."

"Hell, no! Ruza would kill me, and then IsaDora would take my body and dig it under her rose garden for fertilizer. Absolutely not."

"At least Balasi hasn't declined the mission, or her role in it."

"I'm a little surprised she hasn't. I expected her to resign from Quest. But there was no mention of walking out on the agency or the mission. Just her demand that Ruza be removed from Le Mystère, and my promise to care for her."

"This will work out like we planned. We've thought this through. It will work."

"I have news that Petrov's men will make their move on Casmir in the next couple of days. Did you pick up the one Fourtier caught spying on the cabin?"

"His name's Anton Candulee, and he's on his way to D.C. as we speak. We'll try to get some information out of him, but you and I both know that Petrov's men are damn loyal to him."

"I guess phase two has started. In a few days I'll know if I did the right thing. Damn, I hope so, Adolf. I couldn't live with this if it turned sour."

Chapter 11

The ride into Le Mystère was strained. Pierce had tried at conversation, but what he'd learned since last night was that Casmir was short on forgiveness. He was still in the doghouse, and would no doubt stay there throughout the entire mission.

He'd given up trying to talk to her a mile back and turned the radio on. When she'd turned it off a second later, he'd lit up a cigarette, deciding to let her cool off in silence.

Good thing the Jeep he'd rented was open since the heat was damn close to a hundred in the shade, and the steam rolling off his passenger had raised his discomfort level another twenty degrees.

He pulled up in front of the local grocery store

and gas station. When he climbed out, he noticed she didn't.

"Come on, it's showtime."

She gave him a cold stare.

"It was your idea that we look like a happy couple. Tyrel Jenkins over there across the street is gawkin'. If you don't want him spreading a rumor that there's trouble in paradise, I'd paste a smile on that pretty face of yours and start acting deliriously happy."

"Delirious. Now there's a word. Heat stroke is another."

"That's two words."

She glowered at him and climbed out. As she walked past him, she said, "Even happy couples have disagreements, Pierce. Today we're having one, and if anyone makes a comment, I'll tell them I just caught my fiancé in a lie and I'm rethinking the honeymoon."

She had a quick tongue on her, but then he knew that from their time together in Austria. What he'd overlooked back then was how damn beautiful she was no matter how she was dressed or whose ass she was chewing.

As far as he knew she hadn't called Polax, and even though she was pissed about being kept in the dark, she was going to go through with the mission. What worried him was what she was keeping to herself about Petrov.

He had promised her she wouldn't end up a victim in this game. He would keep that promise.

There was no way he was going to leave her behind after he got his hands on the data.

By the time he stepped into the grocery store, she had the counter covered with food. He watched her as she tossed a few frozen pizzas on the growing pile, then a package of cookies.

He walked to the counter and picked up the cookies, crazy-looking pink marshmallow delights. As she tossed a pound of chocolate to the stack along with a dozen candy bars, he said, "You eat junk food? Where do you put it?"

She glowered at him as he sent his eyes over her slender curves. "Maybe if I gain a few pounds in the wrong places Yurii won't be so excited to see me."

"Somehow I don't think that's going to happen." He gestured to the cookies as he set them back down. "Interesting choice."

"They remind me of a pair of shoes I once had. I had to leave them behind on a job in Romania. I had to escape out the window, and the ledge was sixteen stories up."

"Did you have to cut and run a lot?"

"A time or two. Surprised?"

"Nothing about you would surprise me, *amant.*"

"Well if it isn't Pierce and *da* blond bird. I expected *da* bird would have flown *da* nest by now after she saw your humble home, Handsome."

Pierce turned to see Linet standing in the doorway. She had on a skintight pink T-shirt sporting the words Grab and Go. He glanced at Casmir and noticed her jaw was set. Hell only knew what she was going to say or do. She wasn't in the mood for Linet today.

He reached out and put his arm around Casmir and drew her to his side. Smiling at Linet, he said, "Cass loves the cabin. Don't you, *amant?* She's already calling it home sweet home."

He felt her tense, expected the worst. What he got was her hand slipping around his waist as she said, "When Pierce is near it doesn't matter where we are, as long as there's a bed."

He was just starting to relax when Linet countered, and set the tone for the silent drive back to the cabin.

"I can't argue with *dat, cher.* He's got *da* stamina of a bull, and enough horn *ta* drive a woman into a fit of screamin'."

"A hard-drivin' bull," Casmir agreed. "That's Pierce."

"Well, catchya later. I'm on my way *ta* work. If you've got some time, Mr. Bull, come by and see me. You, too, *cher,* if you can take *da* heat."

Casmir had kept quiet while Pierce had paid for the groceries, and she had managed to keep the silence going over half the way home.

Home… The heat must be making her hallucinate.

"You should have told me she was one of your playthings. You made me look like a fool."

"Linny speaks before she thinks."

Casmir glared at him as she held her hair to keep

it from blowing into her eyes. "I don't care about *Linny's* bad manners, or your sad taste in women. What I care about is getting out of this sorry little town. When did you say Yurii was going to *rescue* me? Maybe I should give him a call and get this damn mission started."

"Anxious to see lover boy? And here I thought—"

"Anxious to get away from you."

He didn't say anything to that, just pushed down on the accelerator. They were cruising the dirt road as if it were a four-lane freeway, the hot air baking her face and wilting her pink satin blouse.

They had just started around a sharp corner when she heard Pierce swear. She felt the Jeep swerve sharply and looked up. The alligator was the size of a small whale. It was lying in the middle of the road, stretched out like a fallen oak tree. It all happened so quick. The corner, the alligator, and then they were plowing through thick foliage.

The tree came out of nowhere, just like the alligator. Casmir braced herself for impact. Her seat belt kept her butt pinned down, but she was jerked forward as they crashed into the oak. Her shoulder hit the dash first, then her head, before she was thrown back into the seat.

As her head spun and a wave of nausea took her, she could hear Pierce swearing, then nothing at all.

When she came to she was no longer buckled into the Jeep. She was in Pierce's bedroom. How she had gotten there, or how long ago, she didn't know.

She sat up slowly, every muscle in her body protesting the movement. She felt awful. Felt like she'd been run over.

She pushed back the sheet, saw she was wearing only her bra and panties.

"Pierce?"

She stood up, stumbled to the door and flung it open.

"Pierce?"

He didn't answer, and she feared that he'd been hurt in the crash.

"Pierce!"

She was in the hall half naked when the bathroom door swung open and he stepped out wearing a towel around his waist and nothing else.

"What's wrong?"

She felt dizzy. Dizzy with relief. Or maybe it was the adrenaline rush she'd felt in her moment of panic. She backed up, and used the wall to steady herself.

"Dammit, Cass, you should be in bed. You took one helluva jolt."

He scooped her up quickly, and she grabbed hold of him, felt him warm and wet beneath her fingers. He strode into the bedroom and laid her down on the bed.

He sat down beside her. "I'm sorry," he said. "I shouldn't have been driving that fast. I jeopardized your life and the mission. I'm going to call Merrick and—"

"Some things are out of our control."

"I'm usually always in control."

"Usually? What makes this time different?"

He didn't answer her. He stood, pulled the sheet over her. "I'm going to call Merrick and tell him what happened, and that you're in no shape to go forward with the mission."

"I'm fine."

"You're not fine. You haven't been fine since you got here."

"There's no reason to abort the mission. I'll be fine by tomorrow."

"There's a damn good reason. Two. I almost killed you two hours ago, and I think you know something about Petrov that could change the outcome of this mission."

"Are you saying my acting skills are slipping?"

"I'm serious."

"I'll tell you my secrets, if you tell me yours."

"I'm not in the mood for word games. If you don't want to tell me what you're hiding, at least tell Polax. He wouldn't allow you to continue with this if he thought you were going to end up dead."

"That sounds like you're hiding something more from me. Are you?"

He didn't answer.

Casmir changed the subject. "Mama and Lazie aren't back yet?"

"No. But they should be soon."

"Then maybe you should get dressed." She eyed his bare chest and flat stomach, reminded of what Linet had said at the grocery store. "I'm fine here if you'd like to take a drive back in to town to visit... *Linny.*"

"She's an old friend, nothing more."

"I think she's more than a friend. She can't forget the bull's stamina or his nice horn."

"You've got a sharp tongue, *amant.*"

"It's part of my charm."

"Tell me what you didn't put in your report about Petrov."

"You two have more in common than you know. He's got a nice horn, too."

"What else?" His tone was flat, his jaw set.

"Look, I'm not going to turn chicken. Your commander is wrong if he thinks that's my style. A yellow strip down my back would clash with my wardrobe. It's also a bad color for my complexion. Now, get dressed."

Ruza had gotten more than one stare when she had entered Bubba's. Maybe it was her pale gray satin shift, or the fact that Lazie was strutting like a peacock.

He was right about one thing, however. The ribs were served with a smile and were the best she'd ever tasted.

It was funny. She'd been to lavish parties all over Europe and here she was enjoying barbecue ribs with a rogue who hadn't quit grinning since he'd ushered her through the door and pointed her in the direction of the bathroom.

Bubba's was a rustic good-time place with smiling faces and lots of laughter. Ruza studied the crowd, then Lazie, who hadn't taken his eyes off her.

"Are you expecting me to change color? You shouldn't stare so much, Lazie."

"I can't help myself, *mon coeur*. Casmir's father…he's a lucky man."

"Jacko died many years ago."

"It's still painful to talk about?"

"I don't know you well enough to share my personal history."

"Secrets to guard?"

"If I do, they're mine, no one else's. When you get to my age there is plenty of history."

"The sayin' goes *dat* youth keeps a man guessin'. Experience holds a man's interest."

"And just what exactly are you interested in, Lazie?"

His grin widened. "*Everytin' dat's* made you who you are. Tell me about your life in Europe."

"I don't think so."

"Pierce says you're a stage actress."

"Retired actress."

"So what do you do now *dat* you're retired?"

"I travel, and do a little charity work."

"I haven't traveled in years."

"Why?"

"The Glitterbug keeps me busy. Do you travel alone, Ruza-a…?"

"Sometimes, but I have friends who accompany me from time to time."

"Men friends?"

"If you're asking if there's anyone special, the answer is no."

"*Dat's* a comfort."

"Lazie, I'm not going to let you mess with me."

"Mess with you?"

"You know what I mean."

"*Oui.* But it wouldn't be messy, I promise you *dat.*"

Ruza looked at her watch. "I think we should be getting back. I don't want Cassie to worry."

"Whatever you say, *ma douce amie.*"

He stood, reached into his pocket and tossed several bills on the table. It was far more than what the meal had cost, and that surprised her. Lazie didn't look flushed, by any means. He looked like a paycheck-to-paycheck man with a mortgage.

But there was something, something about him that told her she wasn't the only one with a secret. Saber Lazie was more than he appeared to be.

They left Bubba's and started back to the boat.

Yes, experience was knowledge, but so was being able to read your opponent. That was why when Lazie reached out to squeeze her ass, Ruza sensed it was going to happen. She spun right, the move quick and efficient. Her leg extension on target, she made contact with Lazie's stomach dead center. It took him completely off guard and the force lifted him off the dock like a stiff wind. He went swimming and came up sputtering.

When he dragged himself back on the dock, he asked, "What kind of move was *dat?*"

"It was nothing special."

"*Da* hell. Where did you learn *ta* do *dat?*"

"I'm an actress, remember? Another thing to remember, Lazie, is that my ass is mine. If I want your hand there, I'll send you an invitation."

After dark, Pierce and Lazie took a walk. They discussed the welcome party they would offer Petrov's men once they made their move, how the plan would work out, and then they speculated on the outcome.

Pierce said, "Before they get here, I want you to take Ruza and go to New Orleans. I want her out of here tomorrow afternoon."

"Maybe I'll invite her to see the sights, then take her to my place in *da* Quarter." He rubbed his belly. "I'll tell her it's a peace offerin'."

Pierce glanced at the way Lazie was rubbing his belly. "Something happen I should know about?"

"I didn't know stage actresses were so athletic."

"Meaning?"

"Nothin'. How's *da fille* feelin'? *Da* Jeep *don* look too good. Lucky you both wasn't killed."

Pierce lit a cigarette. "I was driving too fast."

"She say somethin' *ta* piss you off again?"

"I don't remember. If she's not chewing on my ass, I'm chewing on hers. Anyway, expect the unexpected from Ruza. She'll get suspicious when you don't bring her back to the cabin. Be prepared for that. I'll make contact once Casmir has been kidnapped."

"This is a shitty game, *mon ami.*"

"I'm in agreement on that. Cass knows more about Yurii than she's saying."

"And it ain't good?"

"No. I don't think it's good at all. Even if I can get to her within a matter of hours, I'm starting to think ten minutes in Yurii's camp is going to be too long. You should have seen her face when she realized she was the bait. She tried to cover it up, but I could tell she was afraid. She's an experienced agent and has been in tight spots before, but…" Pierce looked away. "Something about this doesn't feel right."

"Call Merrick. Tell him *dis.* Tell him how you feel."

"Merrick deals in facts. I have no proof."

"Can you get her out alive?"

"I have to."

"Because it's your job, or because you have feelings for her, *mon ami?*"

Pierce puffed a little harder on his cigarette.

"I see *da* way you look at her. *Da* Balasi women have a way of touchin' a man's soul before he knows what happened."

"Cass is more than a pretty face, shoes and attitude. She knows her job. She's tough."

"She's tough, but she's also a woman. They *don* see *tings da* same way a man does. *Oui,* the Balasi women are as complicated as they are beautiful, no?"

If Lazie only knew, Pierce thought. "Is the welcome party ready for Petrov's men?"

"It's ready."

"Then all we have to do now is wait for them to take the bait."

Both Lazie and Ruza had gone to bed when Pierce knocked on Casmir's bedroom door. She answered a minute later wearing a black camisole and thong. She looked as though she'd been sleeping.

"Sorry if I woke you."

"I wasn't sleeping yet."

He saw the window open. She must have noticed.

"I was hoping a breeze would find its way to the bed. It's hot tonight."

He walked in. "Close the door."

She did, then slowly turned and leaned against it, giving him a two-second flash of her beautiful ass. The second thing he noticed were the bruises from the accident.

"I've got something for you." He pulled a miniature tracking devices from his jeans pocket. "What will you be wearing tomorrow?"

"I don't know."

"Decide."

"Now?"

"Now." He sat down on the bed, waited.

"I put my things in your drawer. I didn't disturb anything. Just laid them on top." She went to the drawer and opened it.

"It'll be hot again tomorrow. Dress for it."

She pulled the black shift from the drawer, tossed

it at him. "That's all I have, unless you want me to
wear the skirt and blouse again tomorrow. Polax
didn't pack me much."

The dress felt expensive, and it smelled like her.
Sexy and soft. Even his room was starting to smell
like her.

He examined the dress. "We'll slip the tracker
in the hem."

"Let me see it."

He opened his hand and she took it, her fingers
grazing his palm. "One little tracker. Aren't you
worried it could shut down before you rescue my
ass?"

The word *ass* sent his eyes drifting to her backside. "And a beautiful ass it is."

"You don't have to use flattery to get me on board,
Pierce. I've already told you I'm resigned."

He pulled his thoughts back to the mission.
"The tracker is a new design. It's been tested out.
It's reliable."

"It doesn't matter how reliable it is. Yurii will
find it before you find me. He knows I'm a spy now.
Before I'm delivered to him, I'll be stripped, and my
clothes searched."

"You're sure about that."

"I know him. He won't ever trust me again."

The information didn't sit well with Pierce. He'd
been on some rough missions, but he'd never had to
use his body, or let someone abuse it past a damn
good beating. The women of Quest gave their all,
and that fact was never more evident than now.

He stood. "I'm calling Merrick and telling him the tracker will be useless. We'll figure out something else. If not, I'll tell him—"

He had started for the door, but before he reached it, she darted past him and flattened herself against it.

"We'll work around it," she said. "It's not like I've never had to take off my clothes before." She opened her hand and examined the tracker. "The problem with swallowing this is that it could be gone in forty-eight hours. It could take that long, or longer, to reach Nescosto Priyatna. Maybe—"

"Maybe what?"

"I have bruises and scratches from the accident today. More than a few. If you made an incision and put the tracker under my skin, then—"

"No."

"No?"

Pierce shook his head, shook off the urge to touch her. "I'm not cutting into you."

"Then I'll have to do it myself. Of course it won't be as neat a job. It should look like a professional sewed me back up. Like I was admitted to a hospital. You know, after the accident this afternoon."

"I'm not carving up your flesh."

"You want to be able to find Yurii's hideout once I've been kidnapped, right? Do you have a better idea besides washing the mission?"

Pierce turned away. Thought a minute, then looked over his shoulder. "Polax is asking too much of you. I have a mind to call him up and talk to him myself."

"And tell him what?"

"I don't know. Two days ago you were just another agent. A mouthy bitch I wanted to strangle in Austria."

"And now?"

"Hell, I don't know what you are anymore. Let's think of a better place for the tracker."

"There is no better place than under my skin. You'll be able to find me dead or alive. And it will ease Mama's suffering."

"I don't follow."

"You know, the family always feels better when they have a body to bury. And remember the orchids. Two dozen."

"I'm getting damn tired of hearing about you dying on me."

"Then it's settled. You'll plant the tracker under my skin."

Chapter 12

Casmir considered where the scar should be. Pierce had said the tracker was a piece of groundbreaking technology. But her experience with technology had taught her the hard way to prepare for the worst possible scenario.

She wasn't convinced that the tracker was fail-safe, but then it didn't need to be. It wouldn't be there long, just long enough to give him the location of Nescosto Priyatna.

She wasn't as good at dealing with pain as her friend Nadja. That meant it was going to take a lot of liquor before she would be able to lie still and tolerate a knife in Pierce's hand against her flesh.

She considered the most convincing areas for a

laceration caused by a freak accident—a laceration that would require stitches.

It was ironic how things happened, she thought, as she examined the dark bruise on her shoulder where her body had made contact with the Jeep's dashboard, and another on her thigh, then the scratches on her neck.

Still undecided, she left the bedroom and found Pierce sitting in the living room in the dark, the only light the evening moon shining through a window.

He was smoking again.

She sat down in a chair across from him. "We need to do this tonight, right? If they're coming for me tomorrow this would be the perfect time. Mama's asleep."

He was staring off into space. There was a whiskey bottle on the floor next to his chair.

He turned his head and looked at her. "I don't think there will ever be a perfect time, *amant.*"

"If you can't do it, then I will. I planned on having a few drinks before we got started, but if I'm the one handling the knife, I'll have to be sober."

Okay, so there would be more pain involved. It wasn't as if she hadn't dealt with pain in the past. She could do this.

"Give me your knife."

He stood, and she thought he was going to pull the knife out of the sheath on his hip. Instead he said, "Not here. Let's go."

"Go where?"

"Lazie has a flat in the Quarter in New Orleans. I'll do it there."

"You're going to do it?"

"*Oui.*"

"In New Orleans?"

"That's right."

"You think I'm going to scream and cry and wake up Mama, is that it? You can gag me if you—"

"We'll take the Eldorado. Lazie's car has air-conditioning. I'll tell him the plan and that we'll be gone until noon. He can tell Ruza we left early to see to the real estate business. Get dressed."

In a matter of minutes they were on the road to New Orleans, the air-conditioning in the Eldorado running on high. There was little conversation. They passed Le Mystère and within an hour they were in New Orleans, parking the car in an alley behind an iron gate crowded with foliage and blooming magnolias in the French Quarter.

They got out and Pierce led the way up a back stairway. It was late, but the city was still alive with music and revelry. She noted the building as she climbed the outside stairs. It was French in design and nicer than she'd expected, considering Lazie and his eccentric tastes.

She was further surprised when Pierce unlocked the flat at the top of the stairs and opened the door. He continued to lead the way, flipping on a light switch.

The flat was decorated in expensive antiques, rich velvet and thick rugs. It was spotless and smelled heavily of magnolias.

"Lazie owns this?"

"*Oui*. He also owns a home on the river."

"The Glitterbug must be lucrative."

"Lazie's been an entrepreneur since he was twenty. He's more than a bar owner. I'm going to make a phone call."

"Who are you calling?"

"Someone I trust. I'm going to need a few things delivered."

He was being too mysterious. Casmir shook her head. "I don't like being the last to know how this is going to go down. I think I've earned the right to be your equal in this, Pierce. Partners should be equals. After all, I'm the one getting cut, and being sent off to die."

"Would you stop saying that. Dammit, woman!"

It was the first time she had ever seen him lose his cool. He looked ready to explode, like a lit cannon with a short fuse.

"I thought you were the Sleeper. The man with no emotion. That's what it says in your file."

"*Oui*, me, too." He rubbed the back of his neck. Walked to the window. After a minute, he asked, "You remember Frog?"

"Yes."

"He and I go way back. I'm going to ask him to bring by some medical supplies. The last thing you need is an infection, *oui?*"

"You trust him?"

"I do."

"Then call him." Casmir made herself familiar

with Lazie's flat while Pierce made the call. She located the bathroom, a modern, almost feminine room complete with lace curtains and lavender towels. The bedroom was more masculine, still underscored with bits of feminine touches. It featured rich browns, accented with gold cords on the drapes and a gold velvet bedspread on a massive bed with an iron frame around it, draped in sheer gold curtains.

A fairy-tale bed, she thought.

Behind a set of drapes was a pair of doors leading to a balcony. She opened the doors and stepped outside. Below was a beautifully lit courtyard.

It was true that first impressions were suspect to reevaluation. Lazie was a romantic beneath his crusty eccentric exterior.

A rogue with a heart. "An interesting concept," she whispered on the warm night breeze.

Her thoughts drifted to Pierce, and she wondered if he had a hidden side, too. Pierce Fourtier wasn't just an Onyxx agent. He had a past, as well as a mother who had left him. But there had been no mention of his father.

Growing up she had wondered about her own father. What did he look like? Where did he come from? Mama said he had died before she was born.

The difference between her and Pierce was that Mama loved her. Loved her every minute of every day. She knew that, and more importantly, she felt it. Pierce, on the other hand, had lived a life without a mother's love.

No wonder he was so careful with his feelings and so guarded with his thoughts. But he wasn't unfeeling. His feelings were just buried deeper than most.

Cutting into her bothered him. He had refused the idea immediately, then after conceding, he'd slipped into a somber mood.

She heard voices in the other room. Frog must have arrived. That meant Pierce would be ready for her soon. She only hoped that she was ready for him.

Pierce let the big man with the backpack slung on his shoulder into Lazie's flat. When Frog handed him the backpack, he offered the big man a sealed white envelope.

"I appreciate your help."

"I owe you more than a few favors. You could have killed me years ago."

Pierce grinned. "That would have been a waste. Loyalty is hard to buy these days. You've always been straight with Lazie."

"Everything you asked for is there." Frog gestured to the bag. "You need anything else?"

"There's an extra grand in the envelope. I'd like you to drive out to the cabin and stand watch tonight. If anyone comes nosing around let Lazie know about it."

"And then?"

"Back him up if things get ugly."

"I can do that. Maybe I should be working for you, *mon ami,* instead of Lazie." He smiled. "You pay better."

When Frog left, Pierce checked the supplies in the bag. Satisfied that everything was there, he went to Lazie's liquor cabinet behind the bar and mixed Cass a black drink—something that would knock her off her feet in a hurry.

She'd said she could match him in a drinking contest, but he doubted that. He'd been chugging hard stuff since he was fourteen.

He heard a door open and he looked up. The first thing he noticed was that she had twisted her hair up, and that she'd kicked off the black stilettos.

She tracked across Lazie's living room, leaving her footprints in the dense white carpet. He set her drink on the bar, and she eyed it with curiosity.

"Not a French Kiss?"

"It's called Spy's Demise. I thought it was fitting."

"You're kidding, of course. I've never heard of it."

"It's for real."

"And you would know."

"*Oui,* I would know."

"What's in it?"

"Vodka, gin, rum and a few other things."

"Sounds dangerous."

"Aptly named for its knockout punch."

"Well, before I start drinking to my...demise, we should discuss the placement of the tracker."

Pierce poured himself a shot of whiskey. "I still think I should call Merrick and explain the situation. Maybe we could come up with—"

"I should be the one with cold feet, not you."

"Because I'm an unfeeling asshole."

"I may have used the word asshole once or twice since we met, but not unfeeling."

"But that's what you think."

"Since when do you care what I think?"

He stepped around the bar. He was out of sorts, while she had decided to stop complaining. They were never on the same page.

Damn opposites, and probably always would be.

He went to check that the door was locked, and when he turned back he caught her sampling the drink he'd made her. She was wearing the black shift and he knew what was underneath it.

"I like lime. This is good." She took the drink with her and curled up on the couch, hiking the dress up to her thighs. "I've been thinking about where I'd like my scar. You know, it's funny, but for twenty-eight years I've been scar free. So I've been asking myself, do I want it visible, sort of a badge of courage, or should we tuck it away and keep it our little secret?"

She was too damn calm, and it was irritating the hell out of him. He was supposed to be the calm one, dammit.

He headed back to the bar and poured himself another whiskey.

"Is the whiskey to steady your hands? If not, lighten up. I don't want a big X marking the spot."

He tossed back the shot of whiskey, then turned around. "On your neck. Under your hair. There are scratches there from this afternoon, and a small bruise."

"That would work." She took a sip of her drink, then uncurled her legs and raised the shift higher. She was still wearing that damn black G-string, and it didn't hide the dark bruise on her hip. "Or here. What do you think?"

What he thought was that he needed another poker-stiff whiskey.

"Finish the damn drink and I'll make you another."

"Which spot do you like better?"

Pierce didn't answer. He made two more drinks for her in the next hour—strong enough to grow hair—and she drank the last one wearing a smile, but she didn't look like she was going to pass out anytime soon.

He said, "Maybe you should go into the bedroom and lie down."

"I guess that means I should lose the dress."

She stood, swayed.

He dived at her and rescued her from landing on the floor. "It looks like one more drink and then—"

"Help me off with my dress. I'm too weak to raise my arms."

He worked the straps down, then helped her step out of the dress. The swell of her breasts sent his heart racing. Her perfect ass and long legs had him growing a hard-on.

She leaned into him. "My head's spinning."

"That's good, *amant*. That's what we want."

"Don't worry, Pierce. After tonight, I'll still love you, even if you make an X."

She was past drunk. He held on to her, pulled her close. His body was humming, and he couldn't have changed that fact with a bucket of ice or a hammer.

"This is crazy," he whispered.

"What's wrong with your voice?"

"Nothing's wrong."

She looked up at him. "You have nice lips. Did you know that? Did Linny ever tell you that?"

"No."

"Good. So I'm the first?"

"You're the first."

"Do you like my lips?"

"Very much, *amant*."

"I like it when you call me your lover."

"Cass…"

"Shh… It's time to kiss me or cut me."

She was going to hate herself in the morning if she remembered any of this.

Still wrestling with the idea of using a knife on her delicate skin, Pierce bent his head and covered her mouth with his.

Chapter 13

The kiss lasted too long and he enjoyed it too much. But that was no surprise. Cass's lips were as sweet and warm as Louisiana sunshine.

He lifted her into his arms and carried her into the bedroom.

"Another kiss, or is this the part I'm not going to like?"

"You liked the kiss?"

"I can tell a lot about a man from his kiss. It's one of my specialties."

"And what did you learn about me just now?"

"That you like me. Like me more than you want me to know."

He laid her on the bed. "Maybe I was just taking advantage of the situation."

"You're not a trifler."

"Is that a word? I think you're very drunk. And that means it's time for me to go to work."

He left her and backtracked into the living room for the backpack Frog had brought him with the surgical supplies from Lazie's infirmary below the Glitterbug. When he stepped back into the bedroom, he couldn't ignore how beautiful she looked. Her eyes were closed and she was breathing slowly, her lovely breasts rising and falling with each lazy breath.

His eyes locked on her flat stomach, lower...

He shook off the image of lying down beside her and pulling her close, of stripping her naked and enjoying her inch by inch.

He opened the backpack, then sat down next to her on the bed. She opened her eyes, looked up at him.

"You know, Pierce Fourtier, you're a very sexy man. And you have a great ass."

"That's my line."

She giggled. "I didn't like you in Austria. You pissed me off. You really can be an asshole, you know."

"I know. But you can rub a man wrong without half trying."

"And what's the secret to rubbing you right? Give me a hint." She giggled again, reached out and laid her hand on his crouch. "Hmm... I think I'm too late. You feel—"

He took her hand away from his pulsing cock. "That's enough talk."

"I agree." She sat up and nuzzled his chin, then trailed her mouth over his warm lips. "What else do you want to do? Do you want to touch me?" She took his hand and laid it on one of her lovely breasts. "It's okay, you can."

She covered his hand with hers and guided him on a tour of her chest. First one breast, then the other.

She would pass out soon. Dammit, she better.

"Make love to me?"

He pulled his hand away. "You don't mean that."

"Why? Because I'm drunk? Maybe this is the real me. Maybe I've been waiting for an excuse to stuff the actress in a drawer. Maybe I'm dying to have you, but I've been afraid to say anything."

"You're not a afraid of me."

"If you say so."

God, he hoped she didn't remember any of this in the morning. She would hate him for sure.

"I think I'm going to have to mix you another drink."

He urged her to lie back down. She sank into the mattress stretched out like a cat waiting to be stroked.

God, she was beautiful.

He left the room, mixed her the drink.

The idea of cutting into her porcelain skin had him looking down at her as he came back with another drink.

He held the glass and made her take a healthy swig. Then another and another. When the drink was gone, he opened the bag, laid out the surgical knife on the end table.

He'd wasted enough time debating the situation. She was right; if they were going to go forward with the mission, he was going to have to make damn sure that he could find her once she was out of his sight.

He turned her head to examine the soft skin just behind her ear. She was breathing slowly, her eyes open, but glassy. The booze was taking over, but not enough to shield her from the pain he was about to inflict.

He opened a bottle of pain pills, strong enough to put her out for several hours. Mixing drugs and liquor was a no-no, but he had done it more than once and he'd survived.

She was a survivor. They would get through this together.

He fed her two pills, chased them down with more liquor. A straight shot of whiskey. She didn't like it. She screwed up her face and tried to sit up again.

"Relax," he said softly. "I'm here with you. You know I won't leave you."

"I'm hot."

He leaned over her. "It's okay, *amant.*"

"*Amant*…we're not lovers. Are we ever going to be?"

"Not like this," he said, stroking her hair away from her face.

But he couldn't help wondering what it would be like to feel her wrap those lovely long legs around him. What kind of lover was she? Did she moan for it? Fight it? Want it hard and fast? Slow and deep?

What was Casmir Balasi's M.O. in bed? What had made Yurii Petrov fall in love with her? Was it her body, or her beautiful smile?

He shook off the thought, pulled on the surgical gloves and picked up the scalpel. Swabbed her neck with alcohol.

He made the incision seconds after she passed out—a little less than a half inch long. Carefully, he set the tracking device, then slid the flat round disk beneath the skin. After he'd finished making a dozen small stitches to close the incision, he made two superficial cuts next to the scratches adjacent to the incision, as if something had raked the side of her neck in the accident.

He was sweating by the time he finished. He stood and left the room. Peeled off the bloody gloves and tossed them as he headed for the bar and snagged a bottle of Lazie's best whiskey.

When he went back into the bedroom, he opened the doors leading out onto the balcony and stepped out into the warm dark night.

He wasn't afraid she'd wake up. She would easily be out until morning. He spent an hour drinking and smoking, and when he'd drained the bottle, he went back inside and stripped off his jeans and T-shirt, then lay down on the bed beside her and pulled the gold satin sheet over both of them.

He lay there wishing he was drunk enough to pass out, but it never happened. And while he waited for sleep to end his torture, her soft breath teased his cheek and kept his body stone hard.

* * *

Casmir woke up with a headache and a warm body pressed against her. She lay still until she came awake fully.

She was in Lazie's bedroom and someone was in bed with her. She turned her head slightly, and felt a tightness in her neck. She raised her hand and brushed her fingers over a small bandage high on the side of her neck.

It was done. Pierce had planted the tracker, and now he was in bed with her.

She rolled to her side so she could look at him. He was sleeping hard and she studied his handsome face, then his tanned bare chest. He wasn't the sort of man she was used to. She'd spent most of her life dancing around rich men with jowls and bellies that had gone to fat. Men accustomed to enjoying the fruits of their political and financial excess. Men with criminal minds, white bodies and soft muscles.

Excluding Yurii. He had taken pride in keeping himself fit.

She'd never taken the time to enjoy her youth, or the attentions of men her own age—the "wild bucks," as her mother had called them, with only one thing on their minds.

She'd been a virgin when she'd been recruited by Quest. And from that moment sex had become a game of survival. It hadn't been real—two bodies tangled in equal passion.

She'd faked her desire countless times, and even

though she'd had orgasms, they had been of the flesh, not of the heart.

That was until she'd met Yurii. He'd pulled her out of her safe box. He'd changed the way she'd responded to sex. The way she'd always reacted to a man's touch.

Still, her time with Yurii had all been centered around a single purpose—to deceive him. And that had brought her an enormous amount of guilt.

What would it be like to make love just because she wanted to? Because she wanted the man in bed with her? Because she desired him?

She raised her hand and stroked Pierce's chest, sent her fingers experimentally over his hard body. His chest was lightly dusted with hair and it was as solid as granite. It was also scarred. She recognized the scars for what they were—Pierce had been shot numerous times in the line of duty. It was amazing that a man could survive so many bullets.

She leaned forward and kissed his chest, kissed the scars one by one, then circled one of his nipples with her tongue. The act left her hungry for him. Hungry for what had been missing in her life.

"What are you doing?"

She looked up to see Pierce's eyes locked on her. "I could ask you the same question. Why are you in bed with me? What happened last night?"

"It's the only bed in Lazie's flat. Like you, I drank too much."

"Before or after you cut me?"

"After."

"So the tracker is in place?"

"Oui."

"What about the couch in the living room?"

"Too short."

"I didn't do anything stupid before I passed out last night, did I? Sometimes when I drink too much I get a little crazy."

"Oui, you did something crazy."

"What?"

"You asked me to kiss you."

Casmir hesitated, then asked, "And did you?"

"Oui."

"And then what happened?"

"You asked me to make love to you."

"And did you?"

"No."

Feeling foolish, she struggled for something witty to say. "I guess I used the wrong word."

"Say again?"

"Never mind."

There was an odd silence.

She sat up, started off the bed.

"Where are you going?"

She turned back. "Shouldn't we be getting back to the cabin?"

"It's still early. What did you mean, you must have used the wrong word?"

"I should have asked you to fuck me, right? For a man like you, the word love must have—" She stopped. "Never mind. I have a headache. It hurts to talk."

"Come here. I'll rub your temples."

He sat up and pushed himself against the headboard, then parted his legs. "Right here. Lie down. Put your back into me."

She studied the open space between his legs, then lay back down, fitting her spine against his bare chest. She closed her eyes, and when he started to massage her temples, she moaned.

"That feels wonderful."

"How's the neck? Hurt?"

"Just a little stiff. What I said before…last night. I was drunk. I—"

"Shh…"

"I really don't expect you to—"

"Fuck you?" He leaned forward, whispered in her ear, "How about if I make love to you? Last night you wouldn't have remembered any of it. This morning it would be a different story."

A shiver washed over Casmir's entire body. A real shiver—an emotional and physical shiver. The kind that made a woman question her sanity.

She sat up and turned slowly. When he kissed her she wasn't expecting so much heat, or the explosion of passion that erupted between them. She responded with another moan, a moan from deep inside.

When he broke the kiss, she said, "It would be nice if you wanted me as much as I want you, but it's all right if—"

"You don't think I want you?"

"I…"

"I want you, *amant.* I think it's time we stopped kidding ourselves and just went with it, *oui?*"

Then he was kissing her again and she wrapped her arms around his neck as he pulled her on top of him.

"Equals," she whispered. "No toys or games. Just you wanting me, and me wanting you."

Her intimate request was followed by silence. Then he sat up and slowly stripped off her camisole to expose her breasts. "Equals," he murmured, then buried his head and kissed her breasts.

More shivers attacked her. She was breathing hard when she said, "It's your turn to lose something."

She watched as he removed his shorts, then slid next to her and settled his warm body around her. Cupping her ass, he pressed her into him.

"God, you feel good," he said.

He was hard as stone, and she inhaled sharply as he began to stroke her, his touch unhurried and full of desire.

His mouth trailed kisses over her cheek toward her mouth. She captured his lower lip and sucked hard on it. The next thing she heard convinced her that it was true—Pierce desired her.

The groan was gut deep, and she moved her mouth over his jaw, then down his neck, wanting to hear it again.

"Don't stop," he groaned. "Keep going."

He let her take control of the moment for a little while, and in that time he surrendered to her. Suddenly he rolled her to her back and stripped off her thong. Slowly, he caressed her breasts, sucked on her nipples, then slid his hand between her thighs.

"You're beautiful to look at," he murmured, his lips moving lower over her neatly trimmed mons.

His fingers parted her and slipped inside her. She inhaled, felt herself melt around his fingers.

She knew he was watching her, watching her response, maybe even gauging it to see if it was real. In truth, it was like nothing she'd ever experienced before. Pierce on his way to making love to her felt like her first time.

It must have shown on her face, because he groaned, then buried his face against her breasts as he took possession of her body.

The moment was pure magic, each one sharing and giving, offering up their vulnerable side to the other.

She pushed him onto his back and began kissing him and touching him. Without reservation, she closed her hand around his thick cock and felt him pulse and grow.

She took her time stroking him and loving him. She suddenly wanted to know everything about him—the Sleeper who kept his emotions in a box.

For once she didn't have to worry about what she was saying, or how she was feeling. There was nothing false about this moment.

She moved her head lower, captured him in her mouth. He groaned, arched his hips.

He was so big. So hard.

In a matter of seconds she was on her back, and

he was fitting himself between her legs. She welcomed the torture of his body moving hard against her, arousing her center. Seeking entry.

She could feel her own wetness, and she arched into him, kissed him hard, telling him she was ready. Oh, so ready.

Everything was going so well until he said, "No condom."

In that moment Casmir had to make a decision. If she went through with this, it was only right that Pierce know the truth.

She said, "A girl in my line of work is expected to make sacrifices, remember? I can't get pregnant. Not now. Not ever."

He looked at her for a long minute, and when he finally kissed her Casmir felt tears sting her eyes.

Don't ever let a man see you cry.

Mama's words came to her, and she fought the tears. It had been her choice to make certain sacrifices, her choice to become the actress at Quest, and now her choice to make love with Pierce Fourtier.

Her orgasm stole her breath, and it sent Pierce deeper in long smooth strokes. She heard him groan, felt his warm seed spread throughout her inner core.

When it was over, he never left her. With him still inside her, she opened her eyes and found him staring at her.

She didn't know what to say, and that seemed strange. She had always known what to say afterward.

Suddenly she said, "I desire you again. Will that be a problem?"

He slid partway out of her, then slowly back in. She could feel that he was still stone hard.

Smiling, he said, "I guess it won't be a problem."

"Does this mean you finally like me?"

"*Oui*, I like you."

"Did you love him?"

An hour later she was curled up in his arms, and Pierce had just asked her the million-dollar question, but it didn't look like she was going to answer it.

He tried again, "Cass, I asked, did you love him?"

"Who?"

"You know who. I've been trying to figure it out. Why you would leave something out of your report after Yurii was imprisoned. What would be so important or damning that you would keep it from Polax."

"And you think you've figured it out?"

"Did you love him?"

"It's bad manners to talk about past relationships in bed."

Suddenly Pierce flattened her against the mattress and loomed over her. "Dammit, answer me. Is that your secret? The one you've been living with? Did you end up enjoying your work too well?"

She looked away.

"Did you love him?"

She locked eyes with him. "Remember when I told you that I can tell what a man is thinking by his kiss? The truth is, Yurii was thinking of nothing but love and the pleasure I gave him when we were together. He's an evil-hearted, ruthless man when it comes to business, but when it came to me he was someone else. Do you know what that did to me?" She shook her head. "Do we have to talk about this?"

"*Oui,* we do."

"Why, because now you've been inside me, and you're feeling…what, threatened? Possessive?"

"Maybe a little of both. And I know that's crazy. I have no right to either feeling."

"Yurii was a man at peace while I was with him. I destroyed that peace. I saw the other side of him, the side no one knows exists. The vulnerable man inside the Russian mobster. I've seen him sentence men to death, and I've watched him cry in my arms. Did I love him? I loved the depth of his love for me and if that means I loved him, then yes. The answer is yes. A part of me fell in love with Yurii Petrov."

"What does that mean for the mission? What will he do when he gets you back?"

"I stole from him what no one has ever been able to take. I stole his heart. That kind of deception is unforgivable. If it were me, I would want to see that deceptive creature punished. Wouldn't you? Maybe even dead."

Pierce rolled off her and pulled her into his arms, fitting her naked body close. After a moment, he said, "I don't know what I'd do."

"We should get up and—"

"Not yet. You said you can't have children."

"Pierce, please."

"I want to know. Was it your choice, or something Polax crammed down your throat?"

"The women at Quest are given a choice, but they are also informed of the risks that come with the job. I couldn't bring an innocent child into the world that way, Pierce. So I made the only choice I could live with."

They shared a later breakfast after making love again. Pierce cooked while Casmir watched him, enjoying the sight of him in his underwear. He was rock solid—a very desirable man. She no longer felt like she had to ignore that fact.

She liked him, and he liked her. No more needed to be said. They had truly buried the hatchet.

"We should get back soon," she said as she sipped her coffee and stared at him across the table.

"Lazie knows what to tell Ruza. We left early to view some real estate."

"A man who thinks of everything. A woman's dream."

He raised his cup. "To dreams and honesty."

"Honesty?"

"Thank you for trusting me with your secret."

"And thank you."

"For what?"

"I peeked under the bandage. No big X marks the spot. Just a neat little line with even stitches."

He scowled at her. "Polax is going to have to give you a bonus for that. I'm going to insist on it."

"A chivalrous man. It's nice to see that some men

who appear carved out of granite have a sensitive side."

"An offhanded compliment?"

"If you like."

"I like."

She stood, walked her cup to the sink and rinsed it out. "I suppose I should take a shower." She turned. "Want to join me? We could be equals again."

"Equals. It's an interesting word choice."

"It means a level playing field."

"I know what it means."

"Want to?"

He stood and walked toward her. Sliding his arm around her waist, he asked, "What do you think?"

"Are you going to kiss me now?"

"Oui."

And then it came. Another kiss. Another caress. Another chance to forget what lay ahead.

One more time, Casmir thought. One more time to feel alive before I die.

Chapter 14

Yurii's men hit the cabin just after supper. Pierce had told Casmir that Lazie had taken Ruza sightseeing and that they must have lost track of time. She had been suspicious of his explanation, and when a scream outside alarmed her that it had begun—her kidnappers had come for her—she suddenly knew why.

She hadn't given much thought to Lazie's role in this until now. He was her mother's bodyguard, the man hired to protect her.

It all made sense now. No, maybe not all of it, but the pieces were starting to fall into place.

A sudden wave of relief swept over her. Her mother was with Lazie. He would keep her safe; she knew that. Mama would be all right.

She worried about having to explain the situation later to her mother, then realized that it was likely that she would never see her again. That brought another wave of emotion to the surface, more guilt.

She wished she had told her mother how much she loved her, and how grateful she was for always being there for her.

Her thoughts were interrupted when Pierce leapt to his feet and shouted at her to move.

Another scream ripped through the still night as he hauled her out of the chair and pushed her through the kitchen door.

"What's happening outside? Who's screaming?"

"I'd say two of Yurii's men just found Lazie's snake pits."

"Snake pits?"

"Lazie has a strange sense of humor. He also takes offense to trespassers arriving unannounced packing guns, with kidnapping in mind."

"But they're suppose to kidnap me."

"But I need time to get out of here alive."

She turned around. "You're expecting them to kill you?"

"Of course."

She hadn't considered Pierce's fate in all this. "Yurii would stand for no less," she admitted, suddenly more afraid for Pierce than for herself.

"Get in the bedroom."

"But—"

"Go."

"Wait."

"There's no time."

"This is it, then?"

"This is it, *amant*."

Her feet felt welded to the floor as she stared at him. She knew she had to move, but she couldn't. She wasn't prepared to say goodbye. Not yet, not like this.

"Cass, you've got to move!"

"But—"

"Stay alive, do you hear! I'll find you. I'll find you, *amant*." Suddenly he grabbed her and kissed her hard, and the memory of what they'd shared hours ago rushed forward. Then the kiss was over and he was stepping back, looking at her with those deep brown eyes as if he were willing her to survive.

"I have one up on you now. Our own little game, remember? We're no longer equals. And you don't like that much. I know you don't. The 'actress' is always the winner. When I see you next, I'll expect you to level the playing field with a big kiss. Now go. Don't look back, and don't make it too easy for them."

Her lips were still throbbing when she turned and scrambled down the hall and into the bedroom. She had only minutes to prepare. She upended her bag on the bed, strapped her Makarov on her thigh beneath the black garter, then wiggled her feet into the black stilettos.

The window shattered, and she spun around to see a man with wild black hair attempting to get inside. She grabbed the lamp off the nightstand and threw it at the open window. It bounced off his broad shoulder and shattered on the floor. Then he was hoisting himself through the window like a ball of fire chasing the wind, rolling onto the floor as she scrambled around the bed to get away.

She pulled her gun just as the man sprang to his feet and dived onto the bed and flipped off it just as quickly to the other side. He kicked out one leg, knocking her backward. She flew halfway across the room and slammed into the wall. Dazed, she inhaled sharply, and in that few seconds the man was on her.

He stripped the gun from her hand and pointed it at her so fast she had no chance to move. "Too slow," he said. "Women always are."

It was Filip who stood before her. Yurii had sent his brother across the ocean for her. She raised her chin and said, "Hello, Filip. Nice of you to drop in. Still have that chip on your shoulder, or has someone knocked it off since we last met?"

"I never liked you. There was always something about you that warned me off, but I never thought to suspect you for a spy."

"Maybe it was the fact that you were attracted to me and your brother had already staked his claim."

"Or maybe it was my ability to see inside your head and know that you were a lying bitch."

"I think I like my explanation better." Boldly, Casmir reached up and touched his face. Stroking him like a bad-boy tomcat, she smiled, then slowly rolled her hand and raked the side of his cheek with Yurii's ring. It cut deep into his flesh, and she smiled at the fact that she'd drawn blood.

"Something to remember me by, darling," she whispered.

He raised his hand to his cheek. He was furious, but he didn't hit her, though she knew if she were anyone else, he would.

"Go on," she taunted. "Do it. Mark me."

"Alive and unharmed. That's what he wants. But when Yurii tires of this game he's playing with you, I assure you that I will be waiting in the wings to leave my mark on you. Move to the window."

"And if I don't?"

He raised the gun and fired one shot. It splintered the wood a foot from her head. "Then I will have to explain how you killed yourself when you realized you were trapped."

"But I thought you said Yurii wants me alive."

He shrugged. "It would not be my fault if you took the coward's way out."

He had known what to say to make her give herself up. She was no coward. If she was, she would have taken her mother and abandoned this mission two days ago.

She walked to the window. There Filip tied her hands behind her back, then slipped out the window, all the while aiming her Makarov at her.

When he was through, he said, "Head first."

She stuck her head out the window.

"Farther," he ordered, and when she did, he stepped forward and lifted her out.

Seconds later he was moving through the woods, carrying her like a sailor shouldering a knapsack.

* * *

The sound of a gun going off in the bedroom took Pierce by surprise. It was a handgun, by the sound of the discharge. He remembered that Casmir favored a Makarov, and knowing his weapons as well as he did, he knew it was her gun.

"Shit."

Was she all right?

He was about to head back down the hall when the outside door came off its hinges. He sprinted back through the living room and into the kitchen. He entered the utility closet and hit the electrical switch, dousing the lights. He slipped inside, quickly unhooked a latch in the ceiling and pulled himself up into the rafters, then dropped the secret-passage door back into place.

In a full crouch, he listened as the men inside the house moved from room to room, taking it apart. He heard furniture breaking. Shouting. Glass shattering.

"He's here somewhere. Find him."

Pierce heard the gruff voice giving orders. The voice was close. He had only minutes before they found the false ceiling in the kitchen closet. Crouched low, he moved through the darkness, balancing on the rafters as he headed for the hole in the roof Lazie had told him would be there.

He smelled the smoke just as he reached the hole. Since they couldn't find him, they had decided to burn him out. That meant there were men outside watching and waiting. Waiting for him to escape before the flames engulfed the house.

He removed the boards Lazie had tacked up with short nails to cover the hole, then wrenched them up one by one.

The smoke was rising now, filling his lungs and the close quarters around him. He stuck his head out and breathed fresh air, then crawled out on the roof. Flattening himself out, he studied his surroundings. The flames lit up the yard between the house and the woods, and he saw a man to his right shouldering a rifle. To his left was another armed man.

It was clear Yurii Petrov was dead serious about leaving no one alive to follow.

Pierce belly-crawled toward the massive oak at the corner of the house. There he found the rope that Lazie had rigged up to a sturdy branch, and hanging close by was an AK-47. He strapped the gun on his shoulder, then took hold of the rope and swung off the roof and into the tree. From there, he disappeared into the woods and headed for the flat-bottom boat Lazie had left for him hidden in the bayou.

He turned back once as a bright flash lit up the sky. The cabin was an inferno now, a blaze of orange flames reaching for the stars.

Casmir tried to keep track of time as she was carried through the woods. Finally Filip stopped and slid her off his shoulder.

She heard a noise, spun around and saw Nasty Nicky coming toward them from an old sagging dock.

Filip said, "I want Fourtier dead. Make sure of it."

Nicky nodded. "Right away."

"I want confirmation. His ears, a fucking hand. Something." Filip grabbed Nicky by the front of his shirt. "No mistakes this time."

When he released Nicky, he gave him a hard shove, then wrenched Casmir by the arm and marched her toward the dock.

Behind her she heard Nicky say, "I'll find him. I'll call you as soon as he's dead."

"Sach and Moor are coming with me in case I run into trouble on the river. You can keep Gavril to help you tie up the loose ends. And pull out Boris and Maks from the snake pits. Toss them in the water for fish food. Sink them. No evidence, remember?"

They had lost two men to Lazie's snake pits. Casmir shivered, unable to imagine such a terrible death.

Filip, on the other hand, made no comment on the fate of his men, only that their identities vanish at the bottom of the swamp.

No, Filip's eyes were fully on her now, and getting her out of the U.S. as quickly as possible. As he pushed her into the boat she looked back at Nicky. He was still standing on shore. He raised his hand and waved.

Pierce arrived in New Orleans within the hour. He took the stairs three at a time and knocked at Lazie's door in the French Quarter—where he had taken Ruza to keep her out of harm's way.

When Lazie opened the door, he asked, "Is it done?"

"It's done."

"And were we convincing?"

"The snake pit was a highlight for them. The cabin being burned to the ground was mine."

"Shit. They burned you out?"

"*Oui*. Where's Ruza?"

"On the balcony in the bedroom."

"I need to get out of here before she sees me."

Lazie opened a closet door and pulled out a backpack. "It's all in there. Everything you asked for. You're going to keep in touch, right?"

Pierce slung the pack over his shoulder. "I'll call you when I can, but when that will be, I'm not sure."

"Did you call Merrick?"

"Not yet, but I will once I'm en route."

"And what will you tell him, Mr. Fourtier? Where's my daughter?"

Pierce looked over Lazie's shoulder to see Ruza stepping out of the shadows.

"I asked you a question. Where's my daughter? And don't fabricate a story. I can smell a liar as easily as a rogue." She glanced at Lazie, then back at Pierce.

"I don't have time to explain."

"You work for Onyxx. Don't deny it. I overheard you say you were going to call Adolf Merrick. You wouldn't be doing that otherwise. I'm a quick study, Mr. Fourtier. I'd say this entire trip Lev sent my daughter on has nothing to do with a vacation and everything to do with some kind of assignment."

Pierce said nothing.

"I know who she is, Mr. Fourtier. Or, I should say, what she is and who she works for. That's right. I know the truth about my daughter's status at Quest."

Pierce didn't blink. Ruza Balasi was no fool. He said, "I know all about the game you and Cass have been playing over the years. Merrick filled me in."

"And now you will fill me in."

"If you want to know what's going on, ask your brother. At the moment I have a job to do, and timing is everything right now."

"You are not going to leave without detailing my daughter's situation. What has Lev cooked up with Merrick, and how does it involve Cassie?"

Pierce looked at Lazie, who was clearly confused. He said, "Keep her here." Then to Ruza, he said, "My job is to track Cass, and at the moment she's in a very tight spot. This is wasting valuable time."

Pierce again made eye contact with Lazie. "Don't let her out of your sight. Your *mon coeur* is a seasoned spy, and knows every trick in the book."

"If you read my file, then you know I'm retired. That I haven't been active for years."

"And in the intelligence business we all know that holds about as much water as a cup with a hole in the bottom."

Lazie glanced at Ruza. "A spy. No, Ruza-a… Not you. I *don* believe it."

"Why, because I don't look the type? Close your mouth, Lazie. I can see your tonsils."

Casmir sat beside Filip while one of his henchmen drove the boat and the other stood like a sentry with his gun at the ready should trouble appear around the next corner.

The river was narrow and the foliage thick. Casmir kept alert. She wondered if Pierce was out there somewhere watching, or if he'd been trapped in the cabin.

No, he was too smart for that.

The night breeze whipped her face as the driver pushed the boat for more speed. The river was black and there was no moon out. A good night to strike, she thought. Filip had planned well.

The boat slowed and suddenly it was headed for shore. They had charted a route to avoid capture. They would take to the water again, she believed, but it was always a good idea to play rabbit just in case someone had taken chase. She knew all the games, knew the criminal mind.

Filip was no fool. By far, he was Yurii's equal. Though he was at least ten years younger, he'd been raised in the same world. Loyal to the same family.

Still, he was his own man with his own strong convictions. As he had said, if she had betrayed him, she would be dead by now.

In contrast to Yurii's clean-cut appearance, Filip wore his black hair long and spoke broken English laced with an Italian accent. He was built like a machine, and he handled himself like a pro. He knew his job and did it without the slightest hesitation. He wasn't interested in making friends or excuses. He'd come to Louisiana for only one thing—to take her back to Yurii.

She was transported to a waiting car—a black BMW—and the man who had driven the boat was once again behind the wheel. They sped away from the dock, Filip not saying more than a few words to the men as they got lost on the back roads heading east following the coast.

They crossed into Mississippi. This time the boat waiting for them was a sleek white motor yacht.

Filip got out and reached in to pull her from the backseat. Her wrists were still tied and they were beginning to hurt, but she didn't mention it.

She followed the two men down the pier, Filip trailing her. Casmir noticed everything. The yacht had three men on deck, and it had been christened the *Stella di Mare.* Italian for starfish.

The minute they were onboard the yacht's captain set sail.

"This way."

Filip motioned to a stairway that led below deck. But as she started for the stairs, he jerked her to a stop and untied her hands.

"Wouldn't want you to fall on your face and break your nose."

"How kind of you."

"If you think so that would be a mistake."

She descended the stairs and entered a narrow passageway. The yacht wasn't as lavish as Yurii's *Bella Vella,* but it was still worth a few million easy. Filip ushered her into a carpeted stateroom. He turned on a light and she saw that the room had all the comforts of home.

"Take off your clothes."

"Why?"

"I'll ask the questions. Take them off."

He stood there waiting.

Casmir stripped, and as quickly as she shed her clothes and shoes, he took them from her.

"What are the bruises from?" He stepped forward and grabbed her by the hair and examined the stitches on her neck. "New boyfriend like to play rough?"

"I was in an accident."

He let go of her hair and stepped back. Before he left, he gave her a slow head-to-toe. Filip might be all business, but he was still a man.

Chapter 15

Ruza located the telephone in the living room and was about to make a call when Lazie intercepted her, and stripped the phone out of her hand.

She spun around and faced him. "I'm calling Lev. Now give me the phone."

"Lev Polax is your brother?"

"My half brother. The one I'm going to kill next time I see him." Ruza held out her hand. "Now give me the phone, Lazie."

"Not until we talk, *ma douce amie*. You can't stop *dis*. She is already in *dere* hands."

"Whose hands?"

"It's a long story."

"Then get to it."

"I think you should go first. Are you really a spy?"

"Yes, but that can wait. My daughter is in some kind of trouble. We do not have all night."

"Still, Ruza-a…you will explain this lie you have been living."

Ruza swore in Russian, then walked to the window and looked out over the French Quarter. It was well past ten and she was worried. She had never gotten used to the worry, but Cassie had been an elusive spy. She had read every report, and against her desire for her daughter to do something else—anything else—with her life, Lev had been right. Cassie was a natural.

She recalled Pierce Fourtier, and what he'd said. He was leaving to track Cassie. Track her where? Since she'd met Pierce, the man had been as emotionless as a toad. But tonight he seemed anxious. Anxious and as worried as she was.

Why?

In Prague, Lev had told her that he wanted Cassie out of the country. That someone had discovered her identity and that she would need to accompany Cassie since it appeared she had also been targeted. She'd gone along with the plan, trusting Lev's instincts.

Had this *someone* found them?

Her own experiences had taught her that when you were being hunted, and you had no idea by whom, the safest thing to do was to draw them out. Was that Lev's plan? Had he lied?

He wasn't beyond lying. He'd done it before, always explaining it away as part of the job.

"Ruza-a…you know that Casmir is a spy at Quest, *oui?*"

"Yes."

"How long have you known?"

"Since Lev recruited her behind my back." She turned to look at him, then settled into a chair. "I never wanted this for her. She had so many talents."

Lazie seated himself in the chair across from her. "You didn't want your life for her."

"It's a hard life. Dangerous. I was furious when I found out. But of course Lev knew I would be. That's why he went behind my back."

"Why would he consult you first?"

"Because we are Quest. It's the family business."

He looked at her as if he didn't believe her.

"My mother is IsaDora Polax. The mastermind behind Quest."

"She was also a spy?"

"Yes, and a damn good one."

"And you followed in your mother's footsteps, too."

"Not at first. Really, Lazie, this is no time for a walk down memory lane. I—"

"You said you're retired."

"Eight years now."

"And Casmir doesn't know any of this?"

"I never told her about my secret life behind my stage acting, no."

"Why?"

"For the same reason she never told me, and fabricated that story about her being an international real estate agent. Spies live double lives. They protect those they love."

"And did you know when you were younger about your mother's status?"

"Like I said, spies live double lives to protect their families. Quest was conceived over thirty years ago, although it wasn't called EURO-Quest at the time. It was an experimental project at first. My mother had gotten into the spy business years before, and made her mark in the intelligence world. When she was about to retire, she was asked to develop an academy to train female spies. Do you have a cigarette?"

"You smoke?"

"An old habit that haunts me when I'm nervous."

Lazie stood and went to the bar. When he came back he had a pack of Reds in one hand and a martini in the other. She watched him as he lit the cigarette and handed it to her, then set the martini in front of her.

"Thank you."

"You're welcome." Back in his chair, he lit a cigarette for himself and said, "You were telling me about the academy."

Ruza took a drag off the cigarette and closed her eyes a moment, then exhaled. "It was all very hush-hush. Like a secret society. It was called Praza. For years it was hidden in the bowls of the Kostel Panny Marie Sněžné in Nové Město. It means, Church of Our Lady of the Snows. Years later when the agency came out of the closet, it was renamed EURO-Quest. I've never seen you smoke, Lazie."

"I'm a social smoker. It's bad for you, *oui?*"

"So is crossing the street. Today Quest's head-quarters are below the Vyšehrad. When I was younger I never knew anything about mother's work. Neither did Lev. When we became adults it became a part of our lives."

"How? You don't just decide to become a spy."

"No, you don't. Lev started law school and I pursued stage acting. I did well. Found work and quickly became a common face on the stages in Europe. It put me on several lists to some exclusive parties. There I mingled with some very important, high-powered men. That's how I meet Jacko Ludomir, Casmir's father. I was twenty-two when I met him. I had no idea that he was in the intelligence business. A regular James Bond, that was Jacko. He was working for British intelligence at the time. He was in his thirties, handsome and dangerous to my heart."

Lazie smiled. "I think it must have been the reverse, *amie.*"

"Maybe."

"So you fell in love with this Jacko?"

"I loved what he gave me. Cassie was a beautiful baby, and a loving child. Have you ever had a child, Lazie?"

"I have a son. He lives with his mother."

"Do you see him?"

"No. She took him out of the country when he was young. Tell me about Jacko."

"It was while I was at an exclusive party in France

that we met. I had no idea he was there to pick up a top secret document from a Russian double agent. The document had been slipped into my handbag. I had been picked at random to be used. He planned to retrieve the document during the party, but I got a dreadful headache and left early. That put Jacko in my bedroom hours later trying to recover what the double agent had left in my purse. Of course I thought he was there to see me, but I caught him in the act of searching my purse and…well, enough said about that. I told Lev about the incident, never realizing that he had already been recruited into Quest by Mother. I suppose that's when he got the idea that I could be an asset to the agency."

"And before long you were a spy."

"Yes."

"What happened with Jacko?"

"We met again at another party. Then another and another. We weren't enemies. Our agencies had similar goals. We became lovers and I got pregnant."

"And then?"

"I disappeared for several months, and when I returned to work, I learned that Jacko had been killed on a mission in France. I continued to work, raised our child and eventually retired."

"You said Lev recruited Casmir without your knowledge."

"She had just quit modeling for the second time. She was restless and I think he took advantage of that."

"Does Casmir know about her father?"

"She knows the lie I told her. I said he was an actor I met on tour who had met with a tragic accident before she was born. After Jacko died, the intelligence world branded him a Judas. I never believed it, but I have no proof otherwise." Ruza took a sip of her martini. "How do I tell her that after all these years I've lied to her about everything, and that her father was a traitor to his country and his work?"

"Or that her commander, Lev Polax, is her uncle?"

"The lies just keep going." Ruza took a puff off the cigarette. "I can only imagine what she would say if she found out that her grandmother is the head of Quest. Cassie knows IsaDora only as *Babushka*."

"Grandmother."

"Yes. For years I've wanted to tell her the truth, but I'm afraid, Lazie. Too much time has passed. She'll be furious with me."

"I see the dilemma."

"That's the history of the Balasi/Polax family. None of it, however, is important now. What's important is that I find Cassie. And to do that I must call IsaDora."

"I thought you wanted to call Lev."

"I've rethought that. I think he's up to his old tricks again. I can't trust him now."

Ruza set down the empty martini glass and stubbed out her cigarette. "Enough talk. I'm through with Lev. He's misused his power at Quest for the last time. I've told you where I stand, Lazie. Now all that I ask of you is that you turn your back while I make a phone call."

She didn't know what she expected. But it wasn't Lazie's next move. He stood, sat next to her and slowly enveloped her in his arms. Pulling her close, he said, "You and I are more perfectly matched than you know, Ruza-a.... We take chances, gamble for high stakes, and live life on *da* ledge."

"I believe the word is *edge.*"

"The edge of what? No, I have always liked *da* word *ledge* better. It paints a clearer picture, no?"

"Are you going to help me?"

"What do you think?"

"What is the price, Lazie?"

"Friendship, *mon coeur.*"

"Only friendship?"

"It is too high a price?"

"No."

"Then we are friends."

"Just like that?"

"*Oui.*"

"You're serious."

"*Oui.* As serious and determined as you are to save your daughter from Yurii Petrov."

Ruza wrenched back. "Did you say Petrov?"

"*Oui.*"

"It was Ramon Petrov who killed Jacko." Ruza quickly stood. "Lev is going to burn in hell for this. The man who has my daughter is a Petrov? Tell me it isn't true."

"I cannot lie to you, *mon coeur.*"

Lazie mapped out what he knew via Pierce's information. It wasn't complete, but it was a good start.

"So Yurii knows that Cassie is a spy and that she's responsible for sending him to prison."

"And breaking his heart."

"Then she's been sentenced to death." The idea sent Ruza pacing. "If I'm going to be any use to my daughter, I've got to contact IsaDora and then catch up to Pierce Fourtier." She stopped pacing. "I have to hurry."

"Hurry where?"

"Trust me, Lazie."

"*Bon Dieu, mon coeur.* It has been years."

"We're friends, remember?"

"Call me Saber."

"Saber…please give me the phone."

"Again."

"Saber, give me the damn phone or I'll put my foot in your belly again and knock you off your feet."

"*Oui,* a spirited *ange.* I knew it the day I laid eyes on you."

Casmir woke up naked in the stateroom. She had paced the room wrapped in the bedsheet for over an hour, then collapsed on the bed in exhaustion. They were still at sea, and she knew now that she wouldn't see land until she was delivered to Yurii at Nescosto Priyatna.

She climbed off the bed and secured the bedsheet around her. There was no sense pacing. She looked out the window over the bed. It was daylight now. She had no idea how long she had slept.

The door suddenly opened and in walked Filip with a tray. He set it on the table.

"You should be hungry. I am."

She studied the assortment of fruits and breads on the tray. The two plates. Obviously he planned to eat with her.

"Sit, *signorina.*"

"Where are my clothes?"

"They checked out and you will have them back after *prima colazione.* Sit."

She pulled out a chair and, keeping the sheet around her, sat. He followed suit.

This morning he wore jeans and a black T-shirt that strained his muscular arms. His hair was tied back. He had nice cheekbones, Casmir thought, but not as nice as Pierce.

Pierce. Where was he? Was he following?

The mission's success rested in his hands now. She knew he was determined. Knew where he ranked at Onyxx.

But she also knew Yurii and how determined he was.

She looked at Yurii's brother, and found him studying her as he munched on a piece of bread spread heavily with jam.

"Eat. I wouldn't want you to lose your curves before I deliver you. Yurii wants you looking well when you arrive."

"Are you two close?"

"My relationship with my brother is of no importance to you. He has asked that I bring you to him, and it will be done."

"Do you follow all of Yurii's orders?"

"Orders?" He snorted. "Yurii does not order me to do anything. All he has to do is ask, and if it is in my power, I make it happen. It's called respect. Something a woman like you would know nothing about."

"Where are you taking me?"

"I told you. Home."

"But where is home?"

He grinned. "Anxious?"

Casmir relaxed back in the chair and began to pick at the fruit. "Not exactly anxious, but I'm not afraid, either."

His grin widened. "You should be. When I left, Yurii was in the middle of arranging an interesting homecoming party for you."

"And will you be at the party?"

"No. It will be a private party for two. But the stone walls at Nescosto echo nicely. I will be able to hear you scream."

Chapter 16

Pierce called Merrick and got him out of bed. He was on his way to the airport in New Orleans, about to board a private plane waiting for him on the runway.

"Petrov bit," he said. "Call Polax and tell him the final phase of the mission starts now. Who's my contact? When and where?"

"Ash Kelly."

"Ash?"

"I've decided to let him in on this. He's eager to get back, and I thought working with one of his old teammates would be a good idea."

"He's been out a year. This is no time for a trial run. We've just sent a woman into hell and promised her she'll survive."

"I thought you'd welcome Ash back. You were the one who suggested he take the job in the beginning."

That was before, Pierce thought. Before things had changed. A lot of things.

"Are you refusing him? If you are, it's going to complicate matters. He's already in place waiting for you."

There was a moment of dead air.

"You better be right about him."

"Yes or no, Pierce?"

Normally Merrick didn't give his agents a choice. That put Pierce on edge. Merrick wasn't sure Ash was back a hundred percent. He wanted him to make the call.

"If I don't like what I see, I'm going to kick his ass off the mission, and go solo."

"You're running the show."

That was another strange comment Pierce didn't like. Merrick never gave up his authority. He swore. "He better be fuckin' ready to go when I see him. If his brains are scrambled in the bottom of a bottle, I'll kill him."

There was more silence.

"Is everything all right on your end? You seem agitated. That's not like you."

"You owe me a house. Mine was burned to the ground an hour ago. And there's a problem Polax is going to need to deal with."

"A problem?"

"Ruza Balasi isn't happy with the situation. She knows Polax played her. She's not the kind of woman who is going to sit by the phone to hear if her daughter is dead or alive."

"I thought Saber Lazie was handling her."

"Outside of tying her to the bed that's not going to happen."

"So tie her to the bed."

"I'll give him the message. Where is Ash?"

"He's in Barcelona ready to sail the moment you arrive. Pier Six."

As soon as the line went dead, Merrick contacted Polax. He gave him the good news—Petrov had taken the bait. Then he verified that Polax's mole was still in the game. That confirmed, he hit Lev with the bad news—Ruza was on to him.

"Dammit, if Ruza goes to IsaDora, we're both fucked. Quest's future is riding on this mission, but my sister and mother won't see it that way. They think alike when it comes to Casmir. Shit!"

"Maybe we should have gone to IsaDora with this plan in the beginning."

"If I believed she would have backed us, I would have."

"You're sure she wouldn't have?"

"She took Ruza's side when I recruited Casmir five years ago. Neither one agreed with it. It wasn't until after Casmir came back from a number of successful missions that they began to be less vocal."

"In this business, risk is part of the game."

"I hate that word. Especially when it involves

someone I love. Contrary to what my sister thinks, I love my niece."

"You've told me over and over again that she's good enough to pull this off."

"She's one of the best in the business. She's got Ruza's and Jacko Ludomir's blood running through her veins. I'm proud to be her uncle, and even prouder to be her commander."

"Then trust your instincts."

"I do, and I trust Casmir. But IsaDora and Ruza are another matter."

"The bottom line is there's no turning back now, Lev. So what do you intend to do?"

"Avoid any incoming calls from Ruza, stay out of IsaDora's office and buy a brass-plated cup for my balls."

Pierce flew through the night and reached Barcelona before dawn. He located Pier Six and found Ashland Kelly sitting in the sun on a motor yacht, waiting for him.

After the Greece mission to uncover one of the Chameleon's hideouts—a mission that had ended in disaster—Ash had walked away from Onyxx, while Pierce had stayed.

They had lost one of their teammates during the mission and Ash had blamed himself for Sully Paxton's death. For a year he'd allowed that guilt to eat him alive.

Pierce studied his comrade. Ash's blond hair was past his shoulders and he'd grown a beard and moustache. He'd lost weight, and his skin was sunbaked. He looked as if he'd been living in the desert, dining on cactus juice and sand.

"It's been a while, *mon ami.*"

Ash nodded. "It's good to be back."

"Are you back?"

"I wouldn't be here if I wasn't."

"You better be. This isn't going to be a picnic in the sun."

"You don't want me here."

"I want the man I used to work with and trust. If he's here, then I'm happy. If he's not, then I want you gone."

"He's here, and I'll prove it if you give me a chance."

Pierce nodded. "All right. Have you been briefed?"

"I read the file on Petrov, and Merrick filled me in on the mission."

"Good."

"What will he do to her?"

The question caught Pierce off guard. He hesitated, not wanting to think about Cass back under Yurii Petrov's roof.

"That bad, ah?"

"What's the worst thing you can imagine?"

"I've got a good imagination, if you remember."

"Multiply it by ten."

Pierce felt Ash's pale-blue eyes studying him. He wasn't going to say more. He didn't trust himself, or his voice at the moment. He wanted to rewind the mission. He wanted to start over and come up with another way to breach Petrov's command center and secure the data. But it was too late for that now.

"Let's move out."

Ash nodded, then went inside the wheelhouse of the yacht. Within minutes they were moving out to sea. Pierce checked the tracking device. It was signaling strong, and he discussed the coordinates with Ash. His teammate's specialty was explosives. It was said that Ashland Kelly could detonate a charge in the dark with his hands tied behind his back.

That should give him some peace of mind, but since Cass had been captured he'd been thinking about all the things that could go wrong. That usually wasn't his style. He never borrowed trouble. At least he never used to.

To say Cass had simply gotten under his skin was selling her short. He hadn't slept with the actress; he'd slept with the woman who, for five years, had walked in the actress's shadow. He respected the actress; he felt honored to know the woman underneath....

It was the first time he'd let his emotions into a mission. The first time he felt as if he could lose something far more precious to him than his own life.

It was now the beginning of day two. He hadn't slept but a few hours on the plane. Every time he closed his eyes, he saw Cass touching him—touching him like she was touching a man for the first time. And when he'd touched her... He'd never forget the look on her face. Never forget her virgin eyes. They had revealed more than words could ever say.

He understood now what empowered a man to

fall in love. *Oui,* he was in love with her. Cass had the power to change a man. The power to make him a better man. That was why Yurii Petrov couldn't let her go. He knew her value.

The forecast predicted clear sailing, and the seas held calm throughout the night. They would be able to make good time if the weather held.

Two hours later the weather was still holding, and the sun was on the horizon when disaster struck. The tracking device suddenly went dead.

Casmir woke up groggy, with a stiff neck. She didn't realize what that meant until she rose from the bed and entered the bathroom. Staring in the mirror, she saw that the bandage on her neck had been changed, and that was when she knew she'd been drugged the night before.

Whether it had been the food or the drink didn't matter. The end result was the same—Filip had found the tracker and removed it from her neck.

She showered and dressed in her same clothes. Slipped on her shoes. Although she looked a bit wilted, she was glad she had something to wear other than the sheet.

Filip came for her an hour later and escorted her on deck. The sun was bright, the ocean air warm. She glanced around and recognized the Amalfi Coast. She had sailed the Mediterranean with Yurii for a long month on the *Bella Vella.* They had leap-frogged from coast to coast, dividing their time between Spain, France and Italy.

She studied the coast, recalled the day Yurii had pointed out a beautiful villa set into the side of a mountain—the villa that was now looming in the distance.

That day he had ordered his captain to enter the bay where a fleet of boats rested in an azure lagoon. He had told her the man who owned the villa was once a sad, misguided soul, but that after he'd found love his entire world had changed. He'd said that the man now lived in a dreamland with his princess.

The memory sent a chill up Casmir's spine. Yurii had been talking about himself. This was it—the isolated villa built of stone tucked into the mountain like a bird in a nest was Nescosto Priyatna.

The yacht's engines shut down, and that was when she knew she had guessed right—Yurii's headquarters were on the coast of Italy.

"It is beautiful, no, *signorina?*"

She glanced at Filip. He was grinning. She smiled back, unwilling to surrender to any emotion or fear. "Very beautiful."

"I'm glad you like it. It would be a sad thing to hate your prison."

"A prisoner of beauty. An interesting concept."

He frowned. "I admit you are an unusual woman."

"Why? Because I'm not in tears and begging for my freedom?"

"It would be natural. And I would not think less of you."

"I'm sorry to disappoint you."

His frown turned into a grin. "Either way, this is your home now. You will die here. Perhaps an old woman, or perhaps Yurii will tire of you when your beauty begins to fade and the fire in your eyes is swallowed up like a ghost's whisper on the wind."

Casmir raised her chin. "You should try your hand at poetry, Filip. Your prose is eloquent, but your prediction is a bit premature. I've learned never to calculate the certainty of the future through someone else's eyes."

"I am very certain of your future, Signorina Balasi."

She looked away from Filip, fixed her eyes on Yurii's secret sanctuary. Nothing would alarm a passerby to the fact that this place housed a mastermind criminal.

The yacht began to move again, the engine this time humming softly as it slipped into the lagoon and dropped anchor in the crystal blue water.

Casmir stood at the railing unflinching as Filip pulled his phone from his pocket and relayed instructions to someone inside the villa. When he pocketed his phone, he reached out and clamped his hand around her arm and led her to a telescope that was mounted several feet away from where she stood.

He sighted something in the telescope, then nodded for her to take a look. She stepped forward, put her eye next to the powerful lens, and there, above the high walls, on a grand balcony that jutted out from the rocks over the lagoon, stood Yurii, eating an apricot.

Casmir took a deep breath, pushed back the uncertainty that was creeping up her spine. The air filling her lungs held the tangy taste of salt. She felt

a sudden chill in the air. It came out of nowhere—
the tropical air was as warm as the baked sand that
skirted the coast.

"By the way, my captain is also a surgeon. He
assures me that you will have no more than a small
scar on your neck. He was very careful. Although I
do not expect Yurii will be too pleased."

Pierce went crazy for a moment, then called
Merrick.

"The tracker stopped sending. We're in the middle
of the goddamn Mediterranean and we're fucked."

"She was probably stripped and issued new
clothes. Petrov is no fool."

Merrick sounded too calm.

"She's not wearing the tracker on her."

"No?"

"I put it under her skin."

"Why the hell did you do that?"

"I don't have time to go into it. Now what?"

"Now I call Polax, and tell him that they took the
second bait."

"You expected them to find it."

"We're not dealing with amateurs. Of course we
expected it. Sit tight. I'll be in touch."

Pierce hung up, swearing. He didn't like being
handed the plan in bits and pieces. Had he known
that they wanted the tracker found, hell, he would've
pinned it on her chest.

He sent his hand over his jaw in frustration. What
else could go wrong? he thought. What the hell else?

He had his answer a second later when he turned to see Ash sneaking a nip off a whiskey flask he had tucked inside his pant pocket.

Casmir was ushered off the *Stella di Mare* and led past the stone steps cut into the rocks that separated the azure lagoon from the four-story rock villa.

A narrow footpath curled into the rocks, and she found herself nudged toward a small dock where a small boat lapped the calm water.

The boat was piloted by a tall man dressed in a gray uniform. It didn't fit him very well. The pants were too short, as if they weren't his. She should mention it. Let him know that the last man who wore that uniform was probably dead. Yurii was a hard man to please, and he went through men like she went through shampoo.

Filip helped her into the boat, then sat across from her as the man took up his pole and sent them on their way into the dimly lit caverna.

The waterway was well hidden from the coast, invisible to the naked eye. It appeared as nothing more than a crack in the jagged rocks, but the narrow secret passage had a purpose.

Everything in Yurii's life had a purpose.

They traveled the windy cool cave for several minutes. Casmir tried to calculate the distance, but the twists and turns were deceiving, and she soon realized that there were numerous offshoots—grottos leading to other passages. Perhaps one of them led to Yurii's data center.

Suddenly the boat headed toward a rocky shore. Filip jumped out and then held his hand out to her. She took it and allowed him to lead her down a narrow path lit by gas torches. They flicked around her, and this she made note of, too. The passageway was fed by fresh air. That meant there was an exit that led back to the coast.

They climbed stone steps, a railing of iron caging them as it followed the rock ledge upward.

Filip nudged her ahead of him. It was a long climb, and she wondered as they traveled the stairway why they hadn't simply used the outer steps. Her question was soon answered when Filip unlocked a door with a key and she was ushered into a brightly lit room that looked like an infirmary.

There they were greeted by a woman in her late twenties wearing the same drab gray uniform as the boatman. Hers fit better, however. Which meant she had been there longer.

The woman smiled at Filip, but he didn't smile back. She whispered something, then said to Casmir, "I've been sent to see that you bathe. Don Petrov wants you smelling of rose oil when you greet him."

"You mean when he greets me," Casmir corrected. "I'm the guest."

"You are no guest, *signorina.* You are Don Petrov's property now. A slave to whatever he wishes of you, whether it is pain or pleasure."

"That's enough, Allegra. Do your job with your mouth shut. It is all that is asked of you."

A hard look from Filip sent Allegra into motion

and once Filip left, Casmir stripped and was led to
a shower. Afterward the woman instructed her to lie
down on a table and she was given a massage with
an oil that was heavy with the scent of roses.

Wrapped in a white robe, Casmir heard a door
open. Filip stepped back inside with a syringe in his
hand.

She didn't fight what came next—there was no
point. Minutes later she felt the sting of the needle,
and then nothing at all.

Ruza waited in IsaDora's private office for her
mother while Saber Lazie cooled his heels in the
corridor looking like a man out of his element.

The entire flight to Prague he had held her hand,
and more than once he'd said, "*Don* worry, *mon
coeur*, Cassie is smart like her mother. She also has
Pierce closing in fast."

She'd told him he didn't need to come with her.
His answer to that had been, "*Oui*, I do. I promised
Pierce I would keep you safe."

"In New Orleans."

He had shrugged. "We can't have everythin' we
want. Pierce will just have *ta* get used to plans
changin' like *da* wind. Your brother, too."

A side door opened and IsaDora entered her office. Like Ruza, she was lean and looked younger
than her age—seventy-one, in her case. She wore an
expensive eggshell pantsuit and her white hair styl-
ishly short and modern.

"I'm told you brought a man with you." IsaDora

sat and pressed a button on her desk; the screen on the wall to the right lit up, and a camera in the corridor showed Lazie leaning against the wall. Ruza noted that he was cleaning his fingernails with a knife big enough to gut a pig, or an alligator.

"Interesting-looking man. Your taste has changed, I see. An actor, perhaps?"

"A bar owner in New Orleans," Ruza corrected. "But I suspect there's more behind the scenes."

"There always is, isn't there, darling. So what brings you to Quest? I specifically remember you telling me five years ago you would never set foot in this place again."

"You know why I said that. You could have overruled Lev's decision to recruit Cassie."

"And I would have if she hadn't proven to be such a resilient actress, like her mother."

Ruza had carefully thought out what she was going to say. IsaDora was far more protective of Quest than Lev. But she also loved Cassie as much as Ruza did. "Lev has gone too far this time. He's put Cassie on a mission that she may not survive. I've come to ask you to intervene."

"That doesn't sound like Lev. He loves Cassie, even though you've always questioned that. He also knows that Quest can't withstand another failure. The eyes of the world are watching us."

"Then why would he allow her to be kidnapped by the very man who wants her dead?"

The words sent IsaDora's face into a pugnacious frown. "Tell me more."

"Months ago Cassie's mission was to get close to Yurii Petrov. She was to win his heart, then bring him to his knees. She completed the assignment. Weeks ago Petrov escaped prison bent on revenge."

"I know the mission. Lev assured me the other day that the problem was being handled."

"It's being handled, all right. He has cooked up a scheme to use Cassie to trap Petrov. He's allowed him to kidnap her to learn Petrov's secret hideout. An agent from Onyxx is tracking her at the moment."

"It sounds legitimate."

"I have a bad feeling about this. You know the Petrovs. They are ruthless men. They kill without conscience."

"Are you possibly overreacting because it was a Petrov who killed Jacko? He was a traitor, remember?"

"If you remember, Cassie managed to trap Petrov months ago with deception. Is she not a traitor now in Yurii Petrov's eyes? Am I expected to sacrifice my only child to the same family who destroyed her father in the name of Quest?"

"You have a good point. I'll ask Lev to join us and see what he has to say about this."

IsaDora pressed another button. "Lev."

"Yes, IsaDora."

"Come to my office."

"I didn't know you were coming in today."

"I was called away from home. It's important."

"Could you tell me what this is about?"

"Your sister is here. Either she's delusional, or you have some explaining to do. What was that?"

"Nothing. I'll be right there."

Chapter 17

Pierce nearly choked Ash Kelly unconscious before he realized that what his comrade had in his flask wasn't whiskey.

As Ash lay coughing and trying to recover his air, Pierce took a swig off the flask, then screwed up his face and spit it over the yacht's railing.

"What the hell is that?"

"Green tea laced with damiana."

"What's that?"

"An herb."

"An herb used for what?"

Ash sat up, cleared his throat. "God, you're jumpy."

"Answer me."

Ash hesitated, then said, "It's just tea."

"Bullshit."

"I'm not drinking anymore. I'm clean."

Pierce lifted the flask to his nose and took a sniff. "What's this herb do?"

Ash got to his feet. "Takes the edge off my…"

"Guilt?"

"The shrink calls it depression. Sully was my friend, okay? I let him down. He's dead. I think about that day a lot."

"It wasn't your fault. If you hadn't gotten out of there, you would be dead, too. This damiana…what else is it good for?"

"It's also an aphrodisiac."

Pierce arched an eyebrow. "From what I remember, you don't need that. You were pretty popular with the women. You've got a—"

"That was before." Ash gazed out over the Mediterranean. "I don't want even a woman these days. I've lost the urge."

"The urge?"

Ash looked at Pierce. "Need me to draw you a picture?"

"Didn't mean to get into your business."

"The hell you didn't." Ash shrugged. "It's been a rough year. There were weeks I didn't get out of bed. Too damn drunk to lift my head. But I'm back, I tell you. I'm back." Ash rubbed the back of his neck. "You sure are a jumpy bastard this trip. I don't think I've ever seen you like this before. What made you come at me like that?"

Pierce wasn't into sharing personal business, but here they were talking about herbs, hard-ons and women. Not getting it up could be a problem. He'd never really experienced that over the years, and lately the problem had been the opposite. Cass had kept him in jack-off mode from the first day he'd laid eyes on her.

He'd tried to ignore it. Tried to tell himself it was just a male reaction to a beautiful woman. Maybe he'd always known it was more than that. Maybe that was why he'd tried so hard not to like her.

The thought brought him back to the situation at hand. He said, "It's true I've been on edge this trip. It's not you, Ash, it's me. I'm the one with the problem. I know my job, I'm just not used to getting a mission's agenda in bits and pieces. I don't feel in control, and I don't like it. A woman's life is at stake."

"A woman you care about." Ash looked at him and grinned. "I can hear it in your voice. You got close to her."

"This one is a one of a kind. She dresses fit to kill, and she wears crazy shoes. And she can chew a man's ass off quicker than a piranha. She's not like any woman I've ever met."

"I've heard that before, and when I've heard it…"

When Ash paused, Pierce said, "What?"

"Do you love her?"

"More than I thought possible."

It was true Pierce had never thought much of the word. As a kid, he'd ached to feel loved, and it had made him vulnerable. As a man he had realized that he could live without it. Was probably better off without it.

He said, "The tracking device went dead. I called Merrick. He says we sit tight and wait to hear from him." He handed Ash back the flask. "Here, if you can down that sour stuff, you deserve a medal and an iron-plated dick."

It was after dark before Merrick called Pierce back. He answered his phone quickly. *"Oui?"*

"Head for the Amalfi Coast. When you reach the Gulf of Salerno call me. Stay out of sight."

"How do you know where she is?"

"Let's just say Lev took extra precautions. After all, she is his niece, and he's not into suicide missions."

"I wish I had known the tracker was planned as a diversion. I wouldn't have had to cut her neck open and put her through that for nothing."

"It probably worked out for the best. Once they found the tracker under her skin, they were satisfied and stopped looking for more. Polax tells me that the tracker in her shoe is singing loud and clear."

She was hanging from some kind of hook. Her arms were stretched high over her head, and her wrists were bound, attached to a chain. There was a bright light shining down on her and she was naked.

It felt like she was in a vertical tunnel, or perhaps a narrow tower.

Filip's words returned to haunt her now. *Yurii has arranged a welcome party for you. A party for two.*

"You're awake. Good."

Casmir followed the voice, saw Yurii standing ten feet away on a balcony. He was smoking a cigar and sipping a glass of wine.

"You're looking well, my love."

She lifted her chin. "I would blow you a kiss, but I'm a little tied up at the moment."

He laughed. "That's one of the things I love about you, *Kisa*. Your tongue is as sharp as your mind and as irresistible as your body. Can I get you anything?"

"A pair of sunglasses."

He reached out and pressed a button on the wall and it dimmed the light that was shining down on her. "Better?"

"Thank you."

"You've been a very bad girl, my love. Very bad."

"You would know the definition of that word."

"Normally I cut out the tongues of men who displease me. What do you suggest I do with you?"

"I'm sure you've thought of something already."

"Filip thinks I should kill you quickly."

"And what do you think?"

"I want to hear you beg forgiveness. I want to know why you still wear my ring."

"It's a pretty bauble. I'm a woman who likes pretty things."

"I think it is more than that. I loved you."

"Past tense. That doesn't sound good for me."

He frowned, and Casmir forced herself to smile through the pain in her wrists and the vulnerability of her nudity. "We're both victims of circumstance. Position and loyalty, they can be the death of you."

"Are you saying you never wanted to betray me?"

"I had a job to do."

"And you did it well."

"Not well enough, so it seems. You're standing there and I'm about to die."

"You're not afraid to die?"

"Dying young has its benefits. No wrinkles to worry about, and look at all the money I'll save on hair dye."

He was smiling now. He set his drink down on the ledge of the balcony, then stubbed out his cigar. He pushed another button on the wall and the chain she was hooked to began to lower her to the floor.

Give the girl a lollipop, Casmir thought. The actress wins round one.

When Yurii met her below, he released the bands on her wrists and freed her from the chain. Then he pushed her hair out of her face and at the same time wound his hand in it. Dragging her against him he kissed her hard. It only lasted a few seconds, but when it was over, the look on his face told her round two was about to go to the man.

Up against the wall naked as the day she was born, she felt him slide his hands over her hips, then slowly up her ribs, his fingers brushing the underside of her breasts.

"It's been a long time, and I'm anxious to have you. But I want it to be perfect. You remember how I like it, *da*. Tell me you didn't fake everything that happened between us. Convince me, my love, that killing you would be a mistake."

"A woman can only fake so much. I don't need to convince you of anything."

"And it is that truth that has tortured me for months."

Casmir brought her hand up to his cheek, then she leaned forward and kissed him. "One for the road," she whispered.

Yurii stepped back. "You knew I would come for you."

"Destiny?"

"Yours and mine." He raised his hand and brushed his thumb over the stitches on her neck. "Filip tells me that Quest has used you once more. One too many times, my love. I have killed the man who has done this to you, and now I will teach Quest a lesson they will never forget."

"Pierce is dead?"

"I only wish I had been the one who killed him. Come, I will show you to our room. I've redecorated it especially for you."

Ruza came to her feet the minute the door opened and Lev stepped inside. She didn't know what came over her—she had never lost control in her life—but she lunged at her brother before he could close the door.

Screaming like she'd lost her mind, all she could think about was Cassie out there somewhere being tortured to death by a Petrov.

Her war cry sent Saber Lazie bolting into the room. Ruza got off one good swing that connected with Lev's jaw before Saber lifted her off her feet and dragged her back.

"*Bon Dieu, mon coeur. Dis* is no way to solve *de* problem, Cookie."

"I agree with your friend." IsaDora had come to her feet. "What has come over you, Ruza? I have never seen you so upset."

Ruza ignored her mother. "Let go, Lazie." When he did, she straightened herself and took a deep breath. "You're a liar, Lev. You tricked me, and you tricked Cassie. Your intent from the beginning was to sacrifice her for your own purpose. Deny it. Tell me I have it wrong."

Lev glanced at IsaDora, then back to Ruza. "It might look that way, but I would never carelessly put Casmir at risk. Not unless I knew I could win."

"Win at my daughter's expense."

"Casmir did a helluva job for us months ago. She got inside Yurii Petrov's head, and his heart. He fell for her. Fell hard."

"And this is how you reward a good job?"

"She's the only reason this mission had a chance in hell for success. So, yes, I took the risk. Yurii wants her back, and a man who wants something that badly is vulnerable. Vulnerable men make mistakes."

"He wants her back so he can kill her, you fool."

"I don't think so."

"You don't…think?"

"He could have killed her in Bratislava. He didn't."

"That proves nothing. Did you ever think that he might want her to suffer? That at this moment he's breaking her a piece at a time? How could you put her in this kind of danger? I will never forgive you, Lev. Never."

"Casmir is tougher than you know, Ruza. You're not looking at this as a seasoned agent."

"Don't insult me."

"She's one of our best. She can do this. She can charm her way in and out of any situation she's been faced with so far."

"I've heard that said before. Many of those agents are dead today. Petrov will not be fooled twice."

"Even if he remains suspicious, I think this will work."

"There's that word again. You…think."

"All we need is some time. We know the location of Nescosto Priyatna now. Casmir's job is done. We have someone on their way to rescue her as we speak."

"Pierce Fourtier."

"He's one of Onyxx's best agents and I'm told he's only hours away. There's more at stake here than destroying Petrov and his organization. The data at his command station is priceless."

"Interesting words." IsaDora finally spoke. "And the first I've heard of a plan that involves another agency. Sit down, Lev. It's time for some information sharing, and when it's over I'm going to know from start to finish why the hell I wasn't advised on this earlier."

IsaDora nailed Lev with a look—the one he'd stolen from her for when he was dealing with his own agents. "I said, sit! I'm not only your mother, I'm also your superior." She glanced at Ruza. "Plant your butt, daughter, and keep your mouth shut until I ask you to speak. And you, Mr. Lazie, back in the hall."

While Yurii draped a gold satin robe around Casmir's shoulders and led her up the stairs and out of the tower, all she could think about was Pierce.

He couldn't be dead.

She felt sick, so sick that her knees felt weak and her insides were trembling.

He couldn't be dead, but then why would Yurii say he was, and with such confidence? Had Pierce been trapped in his cabin when it had been set on fire, or shot trying to escape it?

The reality of what his death would mean for the mission should have been her primary focus, but all she cared about was that a vibrant man was gone, and that she would never see him again.

He was too virile a man to die, she thought. Too strong and smart to… She stopped the thought, reminding herself that that description could fit hundreds of agents who had died in action.

Oh, God. Not Pierce.

She managed to put one foot in front of the other as they climbed a series of stone steps, down a long corridor with her knees still threatening to give out. Up several more steps to a dimly lit cove.

Yurii opened the door inside the cove saying, "For you, my love."

Casmir stepped into the room, and scanned it quickly. The bedroom had a rounded ceiling at least twelve feet high. The walls were draped in sheer voile, with gold threads woven through it, and in the center of the room stood a naked sculpture in the middle of a bathing pool. To Casmir's surprise the stone figure was a likeness of herself. The sculpture's arms stretched out away from her body. Water spilled from her fingers, sending it over her stone breasts and down her chiseled curves.

"I call it Morning Bath."

Casmir said nothing, her eyes already fixed on perhaps the most chilling object in the room—the bed. It took up an entire corner of the room on a platform. The octagonal bed was covered in gold satin and surrounded by a gold cage.

It was the largest birdcage she had ever seen.

"I regret that I will be busy for the afternoon. Important business that can't wait. You look tired. Perhaps a nap, my love."

She turned and looked at him. She'd never been locked up in her life, and the feeling of being caged like an animal, even if it was a beautiful cage, was unsettling.

But not as unsettling and heart-wrenching as the news of Pierce.

Alone, yes, she wanted to be alone. Alone to mourn the loss. Alone to cry.

Chin high, she stepped forward, and when she did

Yurii pulled the robe from her shoulders. She climbed the steps and settled in the middle of the bed on her knees and watched Yurii walk to a long stone table against a wall. The mirror above it was large and took up most of the wall, the frame carved in marble. It allowed him to view her in the cage, and as he picked up a remote device that lay on a long table, his eyes found her in the mirror.

"I have learned much about you and your work at Quest. You have made many enemies. A very resourceful little bird. I kept that in mind when I designed this room." He turned around. "Regretfully, I was forced to make sure you did not escape me a second time. So, sweet *Kisa,* consider your wings clipped. You are now mine to do with as I wish. And I wish for you many things, not all of them good, I'm afraid."

With that he pushed a button on the remote and the open cage door swung shut, making a resounding click.

"You are a vision, my love. Rest now, I will see you soon."

He pushed another button on the panel and the drapes outlining a set of French doors floated across them, blocking out the afternoon sun and the balcony where she had first seen him from Filip's yacht. Another button dimmed the lights. One more and soft music began to play.

"I'll wake you in a few hours."

Casmir's fate suddenly closed in around her. Yurii wasn't going to kill her. Not yet, anyway.

She closed her eyes, felt tears surfacing. She watched Yurii leave, and when the door closed behind him, she whispered, "Damn you, Pierce, you made me a promise. How dare you die on me? I'm here. Rise up from the ashes and save me. Save us."

Chapter 18

The island of Capri came into sight late in the afternoon, and within the hour Pierce and Ash were in the Gulf of Salerno. He had been itching to call Merrick, and as soon as Ash dropped anchor, he pulled his phone from his pocket.

He would have all the details of the plan now. He would insist on it.

The conversation went well. Merrick did offer him the entire plan this time. He and Lev had done their homework. They had planned for the worst, for any surprises that might arise, and had executed a few surprises of their own.

A mile off the coast, Ash handed Pierce a waterproof knapsack. "It's all there. Everything you'll need. You sure you don't want me to go with you?"

"Yes. I'll keep in contact."

"My information from Merrick warned me that Petrov could have some pretty sophisticated radar. He could pick you up from your cell phone signal."

Pierce tossed him the phone. "Then wait until daylight and if I'm not back, move out."

"Leave?"

"There won't be any reason to hang around after that. It'll mean I'm not coming back. Hopefully I can get to the data and transmit it out before I'm found. That way at least the mission won't be a complete failure."

Pierce strapped the pack to the belt around the waist of his scuba gear, then flipped over the side of the yacht.

He had enough air in his tank to easily reach the coast. He swam hard, stayed deep. He would surface far to the west of Nescosto Priyatna. He had good equipment, and he trusted his ability. What he wasn't sure of was how well-guarded Yurii's villa would be. The man was no fool, and his attention to detail was the best in the business.

The moon was just on the horizon when he came ashore. He had been hoping that the evening would be overcast. But no such luck.

He stripped off his scuba gear and checked his pack. Ash was right. He had packed him everything on his list, and a few surprises.

Using a sophisticated electronic radar detector, he

started out on foot over the rugged terrain. He ran into an invisible radar screen a quarter mile from the villa. It was the first obstacle, but there would be more.

He soon found a way through the radar, fitting himself between a narrow fissure in a rocky cliff barely wide enough to slip though sideways. Twenty pounds heavier and he wouldn't have made it.

He checked his watch. It had been seven hours since Cass had been reunited with Yurii. He told himself that she was all right. She had painted Yurii as violent, but something told him that he also had a human side. It was that humanity that he hoped she could play to as she waited for him to rescue her.

He had to believe that she was alive. Needed to believe that if Yurii had ever loved her, he wouldn't be able to kill her the moment he laid eyes on her, if at all.

He maneuvered through the fissure, and twenty minutes later crept around a jagged outcropping of rocks. There, obstacle number two awaited him—he pulled up his night-vision binoculars and in the distance, stationed strategically around the villa to the west and south, he counted eight armed watchmen packing heat. There would be eight more, he decided, to the north and east.

It would be a long night, he thought. This was where things were going to get a bit more difficult. Where he would lose time, and maybe his life.

To get inside, he would need to kill sixteen men, or slip past them unnoticed.

Weighing that decision, Pierce flattened out and

began to belly crawl toward the villa. He snapped the neck of the first guard thirty minutes later.

Casmir couldn't sleep. She lay awake, thinking about Pierce. She replayed their time together in Louisiana, mostly that morning in New Orleans when she had woken up beside him, and what had happened afterward.

She had loved sharing that time with him. It had been years since she'd actually been able to be herself. And even though he had asked her a hard question, her answers had brought them closer.

Did you love him?

It was an unnatural love. She would admit that, her feelings for Yurii. In the weeks after he'd been imprisoned, she'd had to deal with that. She'd been too embarrassed to admit it to Polax, or put any of her feelings in her report. She'd skirted that truth, but it had never left her. No other mission had ever been so hard, or so life-changing. She'd even considered resigning from the agency. A good agent wouldn't have allowed herself to fall into an emotional trap on an assignment. A good agent didn't allow herself to feel for the enemy....

Casmir fell asleep crying, her thoughts turning into dreams of Pierce. He was holding her close and loving her as no man ever had, not just as a woman, but as his equal. How long she slept she didn't know, but when she woke up it was with a start and she sat up quickly.

Clutching the gold satin coverlet and satin sheets to her naked body, she glanced around the room. It was

dark but for the spotlights built into the bathing pool—
the image of her in stone glowing in the darkness.

Yurii was seated there on a chair pulled close to
the pool. His shoes sat beside his chair and his feet
were in the water. He was sipping a glass of wine,
his head turned to the bed.

"I was going to wake you, but you know how I
used to love to watch you sleep."

"You've been on your foot too much today," she
said.

"*Da.* It has been a long day."

She saw the remote balanced on his leg. He
pressed a button and the cage door clicked open.

"Come to me, *Kisa.*"

Casmir pushed the door and slid off the bed.
Taking the gold silk coverlet with her, wrapping it
around her, she came down the steps. She said softly,
"I would like some clothes. Could I, please?"

"The closet is full." He motioned to the set of
doors along one wall. "But not yet. Hungry?"

"Yes."

"We will eat soon. I'll have something sent up.
The view from the balcony is beautiful at night. We
will dine outside."

"Please, Yurii. Can I dress?"

He sighed. "When you say please, you know I
can't deny you." He waved her toward the closet.
"We'll compromise. Put on the white sheer caftan,
then come and kneel beside me."

She remembered the routine. Knew what would
be expected of her when she returned.

Casmir walked to the closet doors and opened them. They were wired with a heat-sensitive electronic system, and the moment she stepped inside the dressing room it became drenched in light.

She saw the white caftan in a long line of elegant lingerie. The low-cut sheer caftan had dramatic slits that went all the way to her thighs. It wouldn't cover much, but at least it was something.

She dropped the coverlet and found a basket filled with colorful panties—all of them sheer and designed to cover as little as possible. She stepped into a pair of sheer white panties.

There was a floor-length mirror at one end of the closet, and in the adjoining bathroom, a vanity. She went to the vanity and picked up the hairbrush and sent it quickly through her hair. An expensive bottle of jasmine perfume sat on a silver tray. It was her favorite, and that didn't surprise her—Yurii would have thought of everything. A mist of perfume, lip gloss, a hint of blush brushed on her cheeks, and she was heading back out the door.

She knelt beside him as he had instructed. Took the towel folded next to the chair and laid it out on the floor. When he lifted his feet from the water and settled them on the towel, she took the ends of the thick white towel and drew them around his feet, patting them dry.

She used extra care with his left foot. Yurii's deformity was the result of a shark bite that had taken a portion of his foot and three toes.

"You've had your shoe on too many hours again." She scowled as if they were still a couple, and their time together hadn't been interrupted by his prison stint. "Your shoe has made a sore," she observed.

She felt his hand on her head. He stroked gently. "I've missed your nagging. Rub it?"

She lifted his disfigured foot into her lap, and began to massage it carefully. He closed his eyes, the tension in him slipping away as it always did when she touched him.

"Remember how we used to laugh?"

"Yes."

"It felt good to laugh. It had been so long. I think since I was a boy in Armenia. Do you remember your childhood, *Kisa?*"

"It was quiet. School, and dance lessons. Nothing too exciting."

"I have no doubt you were a beautiful child."

She looked up and saw that he was smiling.

Suddenly the smile was gone, and the pain in his eyes caustic. "I would have died for you, my love."

"Yes, I know."

"I have always taken what I wanted in this world. And once I had it, I always found a way to keep it. I have never feared anyone or anything. But I confess I fear one thing now."

"And what is that?"

"I fear a life without you."

"You were my job," she whispered. "I never expected it to be so complicated."

His eyes closed briefly. When they were again locked with hers, he asked, "Then you did love me?"

Casmir refused to answer, but her silence told

him it was true. A part of her had loved him. Maybe still loved him.

"I knew it that night in Bratislava when I saw my ring on your finger."

Casmir lowered her head.

"You feel ashamed. A spy falling in love with her target. Did you keep your shame to yourself, or is that what Quest plans to use against us?"

Us.... Casmir looked up. "I kept it in here." She touched her heart.

He leaned forward and kissed her forehead. "Help me put on my shoes. We will dine on the balcony, and tonight we will laugh, and love like we are the only two people alive in this world."

It had taken Pierce two hours to reach the manicured grounds of Yurii's headquarters. Sixteen men lay dead, their silent screams a testimony to his patience and deadly aim.

He now considered the villa. Nescosto Priyatna was a four-story Roman-style monstrosity. As grand as a palace and twice as secure.

The structure had been built into the face of a precipice that dropped straight into the sea. Made of stone, the villa had a number of balconies jutting out on all levels. Pierce scanned the layout. Entry would be a delicate matter.

He saw her as he was scoping out the balconies—Casmir was on the fourth floor, leaning against a stone railing. The sight of her stunned him. He wasn't expecting to see her so soon, and looking so...happy.

She was a vision in the moonlight. Dressed in white, her hair moving with the soft evening breeze. Yurii's arm was around her waist and he was also laughing.

Laughing?

Pierce drew back into the shadows and watched for a moment—Casmir's words falling around him like he'd just set off a landslide of shifting rocks.

I'm dead if Yurii gets his hands on me. When you come for me, bring a bag along to pick up the pieces.

Oui. She looked dead, all right. There were pieces of her scattered everywhere.

Yurii handed her a glass of wine and Cass took it. They made a toast. He was too far away to hear what was said, but there was more laughing. Then Yurii leaned forward and kissed her.

Pierce witnessed the display of affection, the length of the kiss, and Casmir's response—not that of a woman expecting to be tossed over the balcony at any moment.

The intimacy between them in New Orleans sparked the memory of her in his own arms. He flinched, wanted to reject what he was seeing, but he knew the truth for what it was.

Did you love him?

I loved the depth of his love. Yes, I suppose I did love him.

She had lied to him. The truth was she loved Yurii still. It was why she had never taken off the ring. And because that love had never died, he could no longer trust her.

Pierce crept closer, making his way down a

flower-lined pathway. He reached the open terrace, found cover among the potted lemon trees and giant statues of ancient gods.

Testing for radar as he slowly moved along the terrace, he stopped near a window hidden behind a veil of wisteria. Using a circular glass cutter, he cut a hole in a window large enough to fit his hand inside. Reaching through the hole, he unlocked the window, then slid it open.

Before he climbed in, he shut down all his electronic equipment—anything that would set off an alarm and warn the household that an intruder had arrived.

Inside, he closed the window, and began to make his way to the door. Room by room he would take the villa apart until he found Yurii's command center. It would take time; no doubt the inside was as well-guarded as the outside.

The good news was, he no longer had to worry about saving Casmir before the axe dropped. Yurii didn't look like he was in too big a hurry to start dicing his fiancée up into little pieces. Likewise, Cass didn't appear to be suffering from anything but maybe a bellyache from too much laughter.

What he'd witnessed moments ago looked more like the celebration of two reunited lovers than a standoff between dreaded enemies.

Casmir excused herself to use the bathroom. Like the bedroom, this room adjoining the dressing room was just another elegant extension of Yurii's wealth and his obsession with detail.

They had eaten Li Galli lobster, and she had let Yurii feed her. She'd slipped into the old *Kisa* he adored. She'd laughed and touched his hand. She'd appeared shy at times and bold at others.

She had made a decision. If the mission was going to be a success, then it would be up to her to find Yurii's database. Pierce wouldn't be coming, and as much as she wanted to avenge his death by slitting Yurii's throat, she needed to stay focused on the mission's agenda.

She pulled herself together, and rejoined Yurii on the balcony. The actress had a plan, and for it to work she needed to give the performance of a lifetime.

Now she would seal her fate and Yurii's with the one thing she knew her jailer wouldn't be able to resist.

"You look tired," she said. "Come lie with me."

"It would be good waking up to you in my arms."

"We can sleep, but…after."

He smiled. "Seducing your jailer?"

"Is it allowed?"

"We were always good together in bed."

"You once told me I was a one of a kind."

"*Da.* No one compares to you, my love."

She leaned close, close enough to whisper, "No one has ever come close to making me feel the way you do."

She heard him exhale a sigh, a release of tension, or perhaps a sigh of utter contentment.

She stepped back and left him standing at the

balcony. As she moved through the open French doors, she wiggled out of the white caftan, letting it drop to the floor. She stepped over it, and without looking back, wearing only the white thong, took the steps up the platform and climbed on the bed.

She knew he would follow, knew that the moment had come to make another sacrifice.

He stepped into the room, his shirt already unbuttoned. He was aroused, and she knew what to do to send him over the edge. She lay back on the bed, stretched out like a cat.

He stood at the edge of the bed, his hand on the cage door. "You are my passion. I have never seen anything more beautiful, or more dangerous."

"I thought you were the dangerous one."

"You shared a secret, and now I will share one. You are my jailer, *Kisa*. I will forever be your prisoner."

Casmir rolled onto her side and stroked the gold satin. "Make love to me, Yurii."

It was enough, and he climbed on the bed and lay down. Casmir kissed his lips, then caressed his chest. She nibbled at his neck. Raked her nails over his nipples until she heard him groan with desire.

Her hand moved lower and she stroked his cock through his pants. On her knees she unzipped him, used her hair to tease his belly while she shoved his pants past his knees.

In a matter of minutes Yurii's shoes and pants were tossed outside of the cage.

He was reaching for her when she pushed him

back and slid his boxers to his ankles. "You first," she said. "I know how much you like my mouth. Let me."

Another groan and Casmir knew she had him. She glanced around the room as she continued to stroke him. She saw the remote on the chair near the fountain. A few more solid strokes, a kiss to seal the deal, and then she was off the bed, moving quickly for the remote.

Before Yurii knew what had happened, she had the remote in her hand and had pushed the button to activate the door. As it swung shut, locking in place, he sat halfway up, resting on his elbows.

"You were right," Casmir said. "I am your jailer. My prisoner of love."

"You really are a bad girl, *Kisa.*"

"You're no saint, my love."

"No, I am not."

"You made a serious mistake when you had Pierce killed. I can never forgive you for that."

"Such strong words. Words spoken out of duty and loyalty to your comrade, or is there something I've missed?"

Casmir didn't answer him.

"Your silence condemns you, sweet *Kisa.*"

"As your actions have condemned you. What is the location of your data center?"

Yurii sat upright. "So that's what Quest is after." He shook his head. "Rethink what you are about to do. Leave this room and you seal your fate. I will instruct my men to shoot to kill."

"My fate was sealed the day I met you, Yurii."

"*Da,* it is true."

"If you ever loved me, Yurii, prove it now. Let me walk out of here with what I came for."

Casmir wasn't expecting him to smile, but he did. A generous, smug smile that sent chills up her spine.

"Filip was right. I must admit I didn't want to believe him, but then I had no choice when he brought me proof."

"Proof?"

"It seems a yacht has been spotted close by. A yacht that should not be there. I was informed of it while you were powdering your nose in the bathroom."

Yurii seemed more confident than ever, and that worried Casmir. But what about the yacht? Was it there to pick her up? Had Polax replaced Pierce?

"You have a decision to make. That decision is live to see tomorrow, or die tonight for Quest."

It was true, Polax had sent her help. Maybe more than one yacht was out there. Maybe there was an entire team standing by to invade Yurii's domain.

"Life or death, *Kisa?* I give you my promise that you will not die if you surrender to me."

"And I can trust that?"

"Unlike you, I am a man of my word. I have never lied to you. I do love you. Dead or alive, I will always love you."

"I can't."

He sighed. "Of course you can't. Your loyalty to your family is as strong as mine is to mine. Filip was right. You are Quest and it is you. It is in your blood."

She had no idea what he was talking about, and she would never know. Their time together was over. It was time to go.

"Where is your data center located? I know it's here somewhere."

"Good luck on your hunt. I will be right behind you very soon."

Casmir slipped on the white caftan, then walked to the open French doors and tossed the remote over the side.

As she headed out the door, Yurii said, "*Do svidaniya,* my love."

It was obvious that he had expected her to deceive him again. That he'd been waiting for her to trip herself up. He'd given her enough rope, and time enough to make her own noose.

With expectation came organization. And what she'd learned from months in Yurii's company was that he was a very organized man.

Unlike weeks ago in Bratislava she had no disguise to slip into, no weapon of any kind to rely on, not even shoes on her feet.

Chapter 19

An alarm went off the minute Casmir left Yurii. She met a guard on the stairwell as she scrambled down the steep stone steps.

The guard was grinning like a fool. He was armed, but the gun was still strapped to his shoulder. Think fast, she told herself. He expects you to turn around and run. Instead, she returned his smile, lifted her caftan and flashed him. His attention was diverted for a split second, long enough for her to drop down three steps, point her toe and kick. She clipped him on the chin, and he wrenched backward. Another kick sent him falling down the stairs. She hurried after him, dodged a futile grab as he reached for her leg as she ran past him.

She was now on the stone path that led to the water channel. There she would find a boat, she hoped. That might take her out of immediate danger, but it would also take her farther away from the data center.

She turned back, found another path, one of the dark passageways she'd seen earlier. It was narrower and seemed to be climbing back up. A minute later, the path ended, leaving her hugging a rock wall. She must have missed another passageway. She heard voices. No time to backtrack.

Along the wall there was a narrow rocky ledge. She maneuvered the slippery ledge, nearly falling to her death more than once. She was exhausted and shaky, her legs aching from trying to keep her balance on the ledge as it steadily angled upward.

She needed a place to hide. A place where she could catch her breath and rethink her desperate situation. It didn't need to be much; a fissure in the rocks would do. Frantically she hunted for a hole to crawl into as she negotiated the suicide path that was really no path at all.

She slipped, and went down on one knee.

The good news was the alarm wasn't blasting as loud. That meant she was moving away from the danger. At least she hoped that was what it meant.

She heard the sound of water flowing as she continued to inch her way along the ledge. Was it getting narrower?

The ledge ended abruptly, and Cass found herself thirty feet above a pool of swirling water fed by a waterfall shooting out from the rocks overhead.

She heard voices again. The guards were coming.

She looked down at the water, wondered how deep it was. The voices grew louder. She had no choice. Die or swim.

She had told Pierce she would die here. Well, this was probably going to be it if she missed her mark and landed on the rocks.

Pierce... She wished she could see him just once more. To tell him he wasn't an asshole. To tell him that she had loved their time together. That he had a pair of amazing lips and that—

"There she is."

She stepped off the ledge and plunged into the water, expecting to feel her bones break as she smashed into the hidden rocks beneath the pool. She held her breath as she hit the water.

No rocks.

Still alive.

The minute she realized she wasn't dead, she began to kick her way to the surface. Gasping for air, she popped up fast. Dazed for a moment, she didn't realize she was behind the waterfall until she swam for shore. She dragged herself up on a rock and concentrated on breathing, on pulling herself back together.

She was alive.

At least for now.

She opened her eyes, and that was when she realized it was all for nothing. Nasty Nicky was coming toward her, with a guard behind him.

* * *

Yurii looked into the mirror across the room. In a resigned voice, to the man hidden in the room on the other side, he said, "Filip, sound the alarm."

"It's already done."

"Then get in here and let me out of this cage."

The door opened moments later and Filip strode into the room. "Do you want me to release the dogs on the grounds?"

"There will be no need for that. She won't get far."

Filip went to a panel hidden behind a picture and tripped a switch to open the cage door. Then he scooped up Yurii's pants, swung the door open and handed them to his brother.

As Yurii dropped his legs over the bed and dressed, Filip bent down on one knee and reached for Yurii's shoes. "I told you weeks ago she was a deceptive bitch and that she couldn't be trusted."

"My wanting *Kisa* back had nothing to do with trusting her, Filip."

"But you were hopeful."

Yurii shrugged. "A man is always hopeful when his heart is hurting."

"You could buy a hundred women."

"And none of them would compare to Casmir Balasi."

"You can't be considering sparing her life. Not after this."

"Tell the men I want her alive."

"But you told her—"

"I know what I told her. I will decide *Kisa*'s fate."

"And the fate of all of us? Who decides that? Now that Nescosto has been discovered, we will be forced to move our headquarters."

"We will discuss that later. Have you seized the yacht yet?"

"It is making an attempt to outrun us, but we will overtake it in a matter of minutes."

"When *Kisa* is caught, bring her to the Meetro. I will meet you there."

Casmir would have dived back into the water but she was too weak to move. She watched sawed-off short-legged Nicky as he hurried toward her. He still needed better-fitting pants and a new haircut. And even in the poor lighting she thought his ruddy complexion could use a face peel.

She said, "Hello, Nicky. Still wearing your pants in poor taste, I see."

"I know you've never liked me, but your opinion of me is about to change. Come on, there isn't much time."

Before she could answer, he was beside her, bending down to help her stand. He wrapped his arm around her waist and drew her to her feet.

"There isn't much time for what?"

"I'll explain later. When we get someplace where we can talk. If they saw you drop into the water, they will eventually look for you here."

She was confused by what he was saying. She looked past him to the second man. He was thin and shifty. He looked like a terrorist who had been surviving on rats. His dirty blonde hair was sun-bleached, and his chin hadn't seen the light of day in at least a year. A combat rifle hung on his shoulder, and his Kydex belt was lined with explosives.

With Nicky's help, she followed the scruffy bandit. In a matter of minutes they slipped behind an outcropping of rocks. There she was urged to her knees and she crawled through a narrow fissure in the rocks and into a tiny cave.

Nicky had just come through the hole when they heard voices. Yurii's guards were searching the water for her.

No one spoke until the voices subsided. Then, keeping her voice soft, Cass asked, "Are you a double agent of some kind, Nicky?"

"No. I just got tired."

"Tired?"

He shrugged. "A woman isn't the only one who is allowed to change her mind. I'm not getting any younger. It's time I retired somewhere quiet where the food is good and the women are generous."

Where the women were blind, was more like it. Nicky was a mess. He hadn't earned the nickname "Nasty" for his sour disposition.

"Is Quest going to make this long-awaited retirement possible? Or did this proposition originate at Onyxx?"

"Your boss can be very persuasive. His deal was hard to refuse. So far he's kept his word. I trust him."

Trust Polax? Not if she was waist deep in shit

and there were a million flies swarming. But Casmir didn't voice her thoughts. If Nicky could help her get to Yurii's command center, then she was willing to delay the score she still intended to settle with him. Pasha was dead, and Nicky was responsible.

Let him think he was entitled to a quiet retirement with a blind cyclops, but she knew different.

She asked, "How far are we from Yurii's control room where all his data is stored?"

"I don't know."

"You don't know?"

"I've never been here until today."

"I don't understand."

"Except for Filip and Yurii, and a select few, the men and women who work here are not allowed to leave. It's how this location has remained a secret for so long. If I had been able to give up the location to Polax weeks ago, your part in this would never have been necessary."

That made sense. She glanced at Mr. Scruffy. He was sitting with his back resting against a rock, watching her. She suspected under all that hair and whiskers was a good-looking face, but it was hard to tell. He was studying her much in the same way she was studying him. But why not—she was close to naked, and frankly there was a lot to look at.

"What's your story?" she asked.

"Name's Ash Kelly. I'm Onyxx."

He was Pierce's replacement. Casmir drew in a breath and let it out slowly. "When you get back, if you get back, tell Merrick that letting Pierce die the way he did is unforgivable."

"What are you talking about?"

"What part of dead don't you understand? If you were called in as his replacement, then you surely know why."

It took a healthy amount of control for Casmir to keep her voice even. She needed someone to blame, and at the moment anyone would do.

Pierce was gone, and he was never coming back. Maybe if she repeated that in her mind a thousand times she would be able to live with it, but she didn't think so.

"You're saying Pierce is dead? When?"

He looked completely surprised by what she was saying. "What do you mean, when? Weren't you given the details?"

"I asked, when?"

"I don't know exactly. I was on a yacht for three days."

"I think I can clear this up," Nicky suddenly interjected.

"Then clear it up!" Ash Kelly demanded.

"While I was in Louisiana, Yurii gave me specific orders. After we kidnapped Casmir, I was to kill Pierce. Of course I told Yurii I would see to everything. I even called and said it was done. But instead I killed the other *soldato* that Filip left with me, then cut off his ears and sent them to Yurii to prove Pierce Fourtier was dead."

"Then he's alive?" Casmir's heart started to pound.

"Last time I saw him he was," Ash Kelly said.

Casmir jerked her head around. "And when was that?"

He looked at his watch. "Six hours ago."

"He's here?"

The change in her voice had Ash Kelly raising an eyebrow. He said, "We sailed across the Mediterranean together. He came ashore a few hours ago."

Stay alive. I'll find you.

Pierce had said those words to her just before he'd kissed her—before hell had rained down on them at the cabin. Now she was silently saying those words to him.

Stay alive, Pierce. Stay alive.

"We need to get moving," she said suddenly. "We need to find him."

"We?" Ash shook his head. "Your job is finished. You were the bait to get us in." He looked at Nicky. "You get her out of here. Hook up with your contact and take off. I'll take it from here. Once I locate Pierce and we have the data we'll catch up with you in Capri."

Another tough-guy chauvinistic oinker, Casmir thought. There was no way she was going to leave here without Pierce. They were a team, and they would leave as one. She was about to tell Mr. Scruffy that when a voice descended on them over an intercom system.

"*Kisa,* I know you can hear me. Come to me.

Come out and show yourself now or your comrade will die a painful death. That's right, *Kisa*. I have a surprise for you. It seems Mr. Fourtier isn't dead after all. Say something, my friend. Express how much fun we are having getting acquainted."

"Aaaaah! Aaah!"

"Come, my love. He will die either way, but it can be quick, or it can be slow. You have five minutes to surrender to one of my men before Fourtier loses a finger. A minute after that, he loses another, then another. You know how the game is played, *Kisa*."

"I'm told you're very good with a knife, Mr. Fourtier. So am I."

Pierce sat in a chair dripping wet. His feet were shackled and his wrists manacled to a shiny silver table that had been crafted specifically with torture in mind. His hands had been spread out on the table. Yurii was damn serious about taking off his fingers one by one.

An hour ago Yurii's brother had worked him over with an electric prod after dousing him with water. He'd hung on, fought the charges frying his insides, but in the end his body had shut down and he'd passed out.

He wasn't sure how long he'd been out. He'd woken up in a cage with a dozen hungry rats gnawing on him. He'd strangled the rats before Filip showed up and took him to a place called the Meetro.

As it turned out the Meetro was Yurii's command center, something out of a science-fiction movie. It was more than just a control room, with the latest technology money could buy. It looked like NASA might look in another thirty years on another planet.

But it wasn't only a dispatch and delivery center, it was also a transport terminal. No wonder Yurii had been so damn elusive for so many years—his own private minisubmarine sat in the middle of the multi-leveled computer dome ready to ferry him to an awaiting yacht anywhere in the Mediterranean.

"It seems *Kisa* is running late. Women, they do try a man's patience, do they not, Mr. Fourtier?"

Pierce saw Yurii pick up the knife that he'd laid on the table. He said, "*Oui,* women. You can never count on one when you need her most. But maybe we should give her another minute or two."

Yurii smiled. "That would be good for you, I agree. But it would be a bad business decision for me. You see, I'm a man of my word, Mr. Fourtier. It is why my people are loyal and my enemies afraid."

Pierce was prepared to lose a finger when an elevator door opened on the level above them and a guard nudged Cass forward.

"Better late than never, as you Americans say. As I said, I always keep a promise. Your suffering is over, Mr. Fourtier. You will die quick. Within the hour."

Yurii took a stairway up to a circular level above them where Cass stood on a platform. Pierce took her measure as the guard nudged her along the narrow ramp to meet Yurii. She was dressed in white, and the damn thing was so sheer that, even at this distance, he could see every curve and asset she owned. Her hair was wet, and she was barefoot.

Before he had entered the villa hours ago he'd seen her laughing with Yurii on a balcony—a happy couple enjoying a moonlit night.

An act? At the time he hadn't thought so. But now he wasn't so sure.

She looked around as if searching for him. Their eyes met, and he saw her frown as she took in his battered appearance. He hated for her to see him like this, but what he hated more was that his capture had lured her into Yurii's trap. A trap she might not survive.

When Yurii reached her, words were exchanged. Pierce couldn't hear what was said, but by Yurii's reaction, it wasn't good. He slapped Cass across the cheek, and she countered the slap by spitting at him. Yurii's hand was in her hair a second later, jerking her forward and twisting at the same time. He brought her to her knees quickly.

Pierce swore, helpless to do anything but watch the scene unfold. Cass was now at Yurii's mercy—at the mercy of a man who had been betrayed once too often by the woman he loved.

It was true, Yurii still loved Cass. But Pierce loved her, too. Loved the sensitive secret side that he had discovered nights ago. But he also loved the fiery bitch, and right now the bitch wasn't happy, and he knew what that meant. Yurii beware, he thought a second before she grabbed his crotch, much like he'd grabbed her hair. Yurii let out a scream, but it was overshadowed by an explosion that took the doors off the elevator and sent metal flying over the second-story railing and into a bank of computers below.

Pierce saw the guard that had escorted Cass to the Meetro suddenly leap over the railing. He rolled to his feet and kept moving, heading straight for him with a knife. I'm a dead man, Pierce thought.

A second later he recognized the guard.

Chapter 20

"You don't look good, Pierce."

"Well, you look pretty damn good. Where the hell have you been?"

Ash Kelly grinned. "Lucky for you I didn't stay on the boat. Lucky for me, too. I blew it up."

In a matter of seconds, Ash released Pierce's wrists from the manacles, then dropped to his knees and removed the shackles from his ankles.

Pierce came to his feet out of sheer will. "I've got to get to a computer. Got to get the data sent to Jacy. I hope he's there, ready to receive."

His insides were still quivering from the electric shock. He stumbled.

"You all right?"

"I will be. Where's Cass?"

"Last I saw her she was…" Ash glanced around. "Shit, where the hell is she?"

There was total chaos in the Meetro now. Computers were burning and smoke was filling the room fast. Another explosion brought down a chunk of the ceiling, destroying more computers.

"More of your handiwork?" Pierce asked.

Ash grinned. "You know how I love to play with firecrackers."

Panic had sent Yurii's guards scrambling for cover. They opened fire on Pierce and Ash, forcing them to flatten out on the floor. Pierce crawled on his belly to a computer that hadn't caught on fire yet, as Ash sent a volley of gunfire in all directions. Pierce began to punch in the code from memory that would leave Yurii's database open to be robbed.

"Is it working?" Ash yelled.

Pierce could hear frustration in his comrade's voice. He keyed on that. "How much time do we have?"

"I've synchronized the charges. Our window is thirty minutes to detonation. When this place blows Petrov's entire network will be scrap metal."

"The code's in. Now all we need is Jacy to acknowledge that he received it. Shit, where the hell is he? Come on, Jacy, read your screen. Do you see Cass?"

"I see her. But you're not going to like where she is."

* * *

The minute Yurii let go of her hair Casmir was back on her feet running. She heard Yurii order his guards to stop her. He still hadn't caught on to Ash Kelly's impersonation of one of his guards.

She heard someone behind her, spun around quickly and kicked out at the same time. It took the guard by surprise and he flew back into a burning computer. He caught on fire and continued to scream while he ran, frantic to save himself.

Pierce had said all he needed was a few minutes at a computer to send the access code. She stopped to search the command center to look for him. He was no longer in the glass cubicle. Had Ash gotten him out?

She continued to search for him. Finally she saw him. The minute she sighed in relief, she felt the familiar bite of metal poke hard into her ribs.

"I'm afraid, my love, the day is not going to end well for you."

"I never thought it would," she said, feeling Yurii's hand grip her shoulder.

"Move. There is another elevator."

He forced her at gunpoint to a second elevator as the chaos continued. He shoved her inside and followed her, quickly pushing a button. The door closed and then they were taking a ride to somewhere below the Meetro.

Yurii leaned against the wall, his gun aimed at her chest. "The ring was a good trick, *Kisa*. I congratulate you on using it. It spawned doubt, and that doubt gave me hope. I thought I had lost you, then I saw the ring on your finger in Bratislava and I wanted to believe that maybe you really did love me. Now I realize that I never lost you because I never had you. Not for a second, *da.*"

He was wrong. There had been moments, and it was those moments that still haunted her, and made her question who she really was. One thing she didn't question was that she'd been wrong not to be honest with Polax. She'd allowed herself to get too close to her work. To feel things she shouldn't have allowed herself to feel.

"You should have killed me at the Kelt," she said, then slipped the ring off her finger. "Here. It's past time I gave this back to you."

"Put it back on. I told you once, till death do us part, *Kisa.*" He pressed a button on the elevator panel. "Filip, are you there?"

"I'm here."

"Bring the submarine to the Vestigo. We leave immediately."

When the elevator stopped and the doors opened, Yurii motioned with his gun for her to step out. She looked around, saw that they were in another narrow channel surrounded by high rocks. Yurii would make a clean getaway now. That hadn't been part of the plan, but hopefully Pierce and Ash Kelly had had time to obtain the data from Yurii's computers.

She wished she had been able to avenge Pasha, but Nicky would get his due one day. No matter who or what you were, fate did not discriminate. She had always believed that.

In a matter of minutes Yurii's submarine surfaced in the channel and the hatch opened. But instead of Filip climbing out of the hole, she saw Pierce emerge. Her expression must have shown her surprise. Yurii turned quickly and took aim.

Casmir moved on instinct a second before he fired. She dived forward, felt the bullet rip into her flesh. Felt a burst of pain that stole her breath. Felt the warmth of her blood begin to flow.

She heard Pierce yell *no*.

Heard Yurii cry out.

Then she was falling as a knife was hurled through the air and lodged in Yurii's neck. He staggered and fell to the ground inches from her.

His eyes found hers and she saw pain there. But it wasn't for himself. It was for her, and the love that he had refused to let die.

He reached out and squeezed her hand, brushed his thumb over the ring on her finger. Then slowly, as his life slipped away, he whispered, "*Da*, a fitting end, my love. Till death do us part."

"I'm sorry, *amant*."

Casmir faded in and out of consciousness. She was aware of Pierce saying those words over and over again. Aware that he was holding her hand, and touching her face.

They were in the submarine. She remembered being carried inside. If Pierce was with her, who was operating the submarine? Was Ash there?

She felt Pierce's lips brush her cheek. Heard him

whisper he was sorry again. Then his voice turned loud and angry. "I'm losing her! Get this sonofabitch moving, Ash."

She wanted to ask him if they got the data, if the mission was a success, but his hands were pushing down on her chest now and she couldn't breathe. Then his face faded and everything stopped.

Casmir woke up in a hospital bed. At least she believed that was where she was. She opened her eyes and saw Pasha Lenova standing over her. But Pasha was dead. Nasty Nicky had slit her throat in Bratislava.

"She's coming around. Finally."

Casmir blinked and when her eyes opened again she saw Nicky standing behind Pasha.

"It's good to have you back, Balasi. You're one tough broad."

She looked at Pasha. "I thought you were dead. Or are we all dead?"

Pasha smiled, reached out and squeezed her hand. "We're alive." She glanced back at Nicky. "This guy is full of surprises. I expected to be dead that night at the Kelt until I learned that he was working for us. I wish I could have let you know. I wanted to back you up on this mission, but it was too risky. It could have exposed Nicky, and he's been a vital part of this mission's success."

"So it was a success?"

"Yes. Polax thought it would be best if everyone just thought I was dead. By the way, I called him and reported in. Gave him the good news first. Then

the bad. That you'd been shot. He's sending a plane
for us. The doctor says you should be able to fly day
after tomorrow. The bullet missed your heart by
only an inch."

"I want to see Pierce."

"Ah...he's not here. He was called back to Washington. He had to leave the minute you got out of
surgery. Ashland Kelly flew back with him. Don't
worry about anything now. Pierce sent the data to one
of their command sights, Nescosto is in ruins, and—"

"What about Yurii?"

"He's dead."

Casmir looked down at her hand. The beautiful
ring glistened back at her like a shining hopeful star.

No one would understand the loss she felt. Those
days with Yurii had been like a dream that you suddenly wake up from. But she was awake now. The
dream was gone, and with it a part of her heart.

Love... Such a mysterious word. Such a powerful, confusing feeling.

"Cass?"

She felt tears sting her eyes. Yurii had almost
killed Pierce. He'd shot her. She should hate him, but
she couldn't. He was more than a criminal, more
than a tortured soul. She felt the need to mourn the
man, not what he was, but who he had wanted to be.
But her guilt overshadowed the moment, and she felt
like a traitor. Felt cold and alone.

Don't ever let them see you cry.

She forced the tears away, and asked, "And
Filip?"

Again Pasha hesitated. "He got away. We don't know how he made it out before the explosion, but Nicky saw him board his yacht. That's enough talking now. Your vitals are strong, but you need to rest."

Her chest felt like it was on fire. There had been no pain after the initial shock of being shot, but now she hurt all over.

"That's it. Close your eyes and sleep. It's what you need most right now. The old Casmir will be back soon. You just need time to heal."

Pierce and Ash had just stepped off the plane in Washington when Merrick called.

Sober and in no mood to talk, Pierce handed the phone to Ash.

"We just landed, sir. Pierce, ah…he's gone to take a piss and have a smoke."

"How is he? Not too beat up, I hope."

Pierce caught Ash giving him a sideways glance. "He's a tough sonofabitch, but then you already know that."

"Tell him he did a damn fine job. Tell him we got it all, everything Petrov had in his database. There was invaluable information on the Chameleon. It'll put us back on his ass. I'd like to see both of you in my office in the morning to talk about it."

"I'll tell him."

"By the way. Nice work on bringing Nescosto Priyatna down. It's good to see you haven't lost your talent. Welcome back, Kelly."

Chapter 21

Three days later Casmir flew into Prague. As she descended from the plane she saw two cars waiting for them. Pasha had been kind enough to buy her clothes to wear. It wasn't her usual style—Pasha had none—but she was grateful nonetheless.

She stepped off the plane, and the two cars were a short distance away. Polax was standing next to one of them. She was in no mood to speak to him. He'd lied to her time and again about the mission, and she wasn't ready to forgive him.

He was smiling. She had expected that, but not the embrace he gave her as he greeted her.

"It's good to see you. Very good."

She winced when he gave her a squeeze, and he

released her quickly. "Sorry, I just… Well, you did a fine job for us. I wanted you to know that."

"Where's Mama?"

"She's here." He motioned to the other car sitting on the tarmac. "She's fine. Anxious to see you."

"You brought her here?" Casmir frowned. "But I haven't had time to prepare what I'm going to say to her. I need to think up a—"

"Don't worry. I've handled it. Come on. I'll walk with you."

As they began to walk toward the car she expected him to fill her in on how he'd handled it. But he never said another word. He was acting strange, she thought. Too kind. And what was that hug all about?

He stopped ten feet short of the car and turned to her once more. "It really is good to have you back. You'll be on sabbatical for a while. We'll talk about the particulars later."

Another hug, this one with a bit more care, but longer. Then he kissed her cheek before heading off to join Pasha and Nicky.

"Wait a minute."

He turned. "I've got to get back to the office. I'll call you."

The black-tinted window on the second car slid down. Inside she saw her mother's face. She looked beautiful, as always. She noticed her hair was perfect, noticed she wasn't smiling.

She should be smiling, Casmir thought. Why wasn't she happy to see her?

She suddenly knew the answer. Polax had told

Mama. He'd told her about Quest. He'd told her the truth about who she was and who she worked for.

Damn him, Cass thought. If she could move faster than a snail in a wind storm, she'd catch up to him and plant her foot in his flat ass.

She looked down at her shoes. Pasha had picked out a pair of conservative flats in an ugly brown to match the drab brown suit. They didn't even have pointed toes. Little damage they would do.

Everything was going to hell in a hurry.

What to say? How to begin?

Casmir raised her chin and smiled at her mother. "Hi, Mama. You're looking well."

"You, on the other hand, look terrible. Get in the car."

It wasn't until Casmir got in the limo that she saw her grandmother seated across from Ruza.

This was just going from bad to worse, she thought. To explain the past five years to her mother would be bad enough, but with Grandma Dora in the wings...

She should have stayed in Italy. She would have lived longer.

"Hi, Grandma." She turned and kissed her mother's cheek, but when she attempted to lean forward to offer the same to her grandmother, a pain shot through her chest and she inhaled sharply.

"I'll come to you, dear." IsaDora slid forward and kissed Casmir's cheek. Then, with her bone-handled cane, she rapped on the inside window and it buzzed down halfway.

"Charles Bridge, Miles. Take your time. We have

plenty to talk about." Her eyes back on Casmir, she smiled. "Now then, I—"

"Mother, I want to go first," Ruza said.

"No, I think I should go first. After all, I'm the one to blame. I started this before you were born."

"Started what?" Casmir looked from her mother to her grandmother. She had expected them to be angry, rifling questions at her right and left. But they looked more nervous than she did.

IsaDora looked at her watch. "I should go first. I have a meeting in an hour."

"I should know better than to think I can ever win a round with you," Ruza conceded.

IsaDora grinned. "Now then, dear. Before you say anything, let me explain."

An hour later, when Miles dropped her grandmother off at Quest Headquarters and she slowly walked up the steps to the Vyšehrad, Casmir looked on, completely speechless.

Her grandmother worked for Quest. No, her grandmother *was* Quest. She had created the agency. She turned back to her mother. Ruza hadn't said a word for the past hour as the car had slowly cruised the city while IsaDora gave her a history lesson on Quest, and her years as a spy.

Grandma Dora a spy? And Polax…he was her uncle?

It was then she realized that Yurii had known the truth about her. He'd said, *You are loyal to your family, as I am loyal to mine. You have no choice. It's in your blood.*

And if he knew the truth, so did Pierce. She would bet her favorite panties that he knew from the beginning every detail of who, what and why.

"I suppose it's my turn."

Casmir slipped across the seat so she could look straight at her mother. She said, "You and Grandma Dora have known what I do all along and you let me continue to deceive you. Do you know how hard it's been to keep this lie going?"

"I imagine about as hard as it was for me."

"But I was the one who—"

"Cassie, your grandmother didn't tell you everything. I need to share something with you, too. Remember when I said I met your father on the stage? That he was also an actor?"

"Yes."

"Well, he was a spy like me. Like all of us. While I worked for Quest, he was working for British Intelligence."

Casmir sat frozen for a moment. "You work for Quest, too? You!"

"Don't be angry, Cassie."

"Angry is when you lose your favorite shoes, Mama. I'm past angry. I'm furious."

"Let me explain."

"Yes, I think you should."

"It was only for a short time. A few years before you were born, and then a few years after. I've been retired for some time, but—"

"You lied to me all these years?"

"I wanted to tell you. I started to so many times."

Casmir stared out the window. She couldn't believe what she was hearing.

"Don't be furious with me, darling. I wasn't happy at all when Lev went behind my back and recruited you into Quest. I was determined that you wouldn't follow in the family business. But Lev insisted that you had what it took to be a spy. I suppose he was right. You've proven that to all of us over the years."

Casmir looked back. "Our lives have all been a lie, Mama."

"No. Our lives have been about loyalty, and not hurting the ones we love. I forgave Lev a few years ago for recruiting you. I forgave him again yesterday for putting you in a very dangerous position. I forgave him because it has brought us here. Together, sharing the truth. We will be stronger for this."

"My mother the spy."

"My daughter the superspy. Lev told me how you saved Pierce Fourtier's life. I'm very proud of you."

"I'm going away for a while," Casmir said. "I'm on sabbatical."

"Lev mentioned that you could use a vacation. A real one."

"A remote island sounds nice."

Ruza patted Casmir's hand. "Not too remote. It appears you need to do a bit of shopping. Moroccan brown looks dreadful on you, Cassie. And those shoes have got to go."

Casmir laughed, then winced. "Ouch. I love you, Mama."

"I love you, too, Cassie. I was terrified for you when I learned what part you were expected to play on this mission. Saber had to restrain me from taking Lev's head off."

"Saber?" Casmir arched an eyebrow.

"Don't give me that look."

"What look?"

"That look. He's just a friend."

"I've seen the way he looks at you, and I've seen the way you look at him."

"For so long all I have ever wanted was to enjoy the memory of your father. Jacko was a wonderful man. He was smart and exciting and... Well, when you get back, we'll sit down and I'll tell you about your father. How we met and how he died. But right now you need some time."

Time. Would time heal the hole she felt deep inside? Casmir wasn't sure. "I have things to tell you, too."

Casmir realized she was again stroking the ring on her finger.

"A spy's life isn't easy, Cassie. The good ones aren't cold-feeling machines. And the criminals we encounter are human, too. They were born with hopes and dreams the same as us. There is strength in understanding. Give yourself permission to mourn your loss, and over time it will heal your sorrow."

"He wasn't all bad, Mama."

"They never are, darling. When you're ready, I'll listen."

"Thank you, Mama."

"You're welcome." Ruza smiled. "Then it's settled. We'll take a trip, just the two of us, when you get back and I return from my cruise. We'll talk and laugh, and...shop."

"You're taking a cruise? By yourself?"

"Saber is going to meet me in Florida."

"You're taking a cruise with Lazie?"

Ruza blushed. "He's been a good friend to me. He has a son he hasn't seen in years. He lives in Santo Domingo. I've convinced him they should reconnect. Call me and let me know where you are?"

"I'll call."

Casmir flew to Crete. Polax had told her to take all the time she needed. Someplace warm to recuperate.

She'd made peace with Uncle Lev. She still had a hard time seeing him as anything but her boss, but she understood things better now. Why he'd always been more indulgent with her moods and her tendency to speak her mind. Why he had wanted Pierce Fourtier to partner her.

I wanted one of the best in the business on our side. I wanted you safe and...I'm just damn glad it all worked out.

Pierce. She hadn't heard from him, but she hadn't expected to. It was back to business as usual for him, as it would be for her eventually. They'd shared a moment. A taste of something beautiful. Life was funny that way. Sometimes all you got was a taste. Enough to keep you going. A little hope until next time.

The Hotel Orion in Matala was modest but secluded. She would spend a few weeks here doing nothing. Regain her strength, and heal her scars.

And she would heal. After all, she had Ruza and IsaDora's blood running through her veins.

Her hotel room was a pastel green, with a balcony overlooking the sand caves and pale cliffs that made the area so breathtaking. She slipped into a routine after two days—languished on the beach by day, and dined on Greek fare in the open dining room in the evening.

There were plenty of men who engaged her in conversation. One persistent tycoon who had a silver tongue sought her out on the fourth day. Dinner and dancing, a smiling face. The distraction was amusing at best.

She wondered who he was. The real man beneath the dark tan and too much gold jewelry. Did he have a secret? Was he here to play, or to forget? Or was he just a rich fool with too much ego and poor taste in cologne?

Whatever his agenda was, she had her own. She was here to get back on track, and to do that she'd taken Mama's advice. She'd given herself permission to mourn Yurii. To come to terms with her part in his death and to celebrate the private man beneath his caustic reputation.

On the eighth day she decided to avoid the tycoon. He had become a constant shadow, and she knew what he was after. She had no wish to engage in an island affair with a Latin lover.

She made arrangements to leave Crete early the next morning. Enjoyed the day on her balcony, and by late afternoon she had decided to take a walk on the beach.

She ditched her shadow, easy enough to do when you were a spy. Some things just came naturally.

The warm breeze felt good on her face, and it played with the colorful green sarong she'd tied around her waist.

She arrived back in the hotel lobby just before dinner and spotted the tycoon at the lobby bar. She stepped into an alcove, then up the back stairs to her room. She slipped inside, noting a heady aroma as she locked the door behind her. She turned and promptly froze when she saw flowers everywhere.

Don't be cheap. I want two dozen orchids at my funeral. Promise me.

On weak legs she walked to each vase, searching for a card. There were orchids in every bouquet, but there were also roses in every color imaginable, from yellow to red, peach and pink.

But no card.

She sat down on the bed overwhelmed.

One thing you should know about me is that I say what I mean. There's no bullshit.

She laid back on the bed and revisited the first day she'd met Pierce in Austria, then the day he'd fought Parnel in the bowels of the Glitterbug, the night he'd planted the tracker in her neck. The morning after.

She glanced at the vase of flowers on the night

stand and suddenly noticed a small white envelope tucked in between three pink roses. Sitting up, she reached for it and ripped it open.

Another perfect day for a stroll. Oui, *the scenery here is outstanding,* amant.

He was here. Pierce was in the hotel.

Cass was on her feet in an instant. She showered quickly, then went through her clothes, this time selecting something with more care than she'd done in days—a soft white silk shift and a sexy pair of strapped sandals.

She had completely forgotten about the tycoon when she entered the lobby. He came to his feet at the bar, and there was no avoiding him. She strolled toward him, searching her surroundings— looking for a tall, dark Frenchman with a cigarette in his hand.

"You're beautiful this evening. Stunning. I've missed you today. Where have you been hiding? A drink, then dinner?"

She smiled. "I'm afraid tonight I have other plans. I'm—"

"With her boyfriend. A jealous badass, *mon ami.* Hit the road."

The heavy voice came from behind her. Casmir's heart skipped a beat. She turned and found Pierce at the end of the bar. He said to the bartender, "The lady will have a French Kiss."

The tycoon looked at Pierce, took his measure. There was a moment of indecision, then he said, "You are a lucky man. I'll say good-night."

Casmir walked to the end of the bar and settled on the empty stool next to where Pierce stood. Yes, he was smoking, and yes, he was as handsome as she remembered.

"How long have you been here?" she asked.

"Are we talking the bar, or the hotel?"

"Hotel."

"Two days."

"And what have you been doing for two days?"

"Enjoying the scenery."

"Have you always wanted to visit Crete?"

He grinned. "I like the weather, and the food."

The bartender brought her drink. Pierce slid it toward her. "What should we drink to?"

She raised the glass. "To survival. There is no road to anything. One thing at a time, all things in—"

"Succession. That which grows fast withers as rapidly—that which grows slowly endures."

"You surprise me. J. G. Holland, too?"

"I polished up on the flight." He leaned in, sniffed her neck. "You smell good."

"I smell like orchids and roses. My room is overflowing with them."

"A secret admirer?"

Suddenly she felt like her life was about to change. Unsure she was ready, she stood. "I don't know. Are you an admirer?"

"*Oui.* A big fan."

"You're a fan of mouthy bitches?"

His grin widened. "It appears so."

She studied his face. He looked good. No, he looked exceptionally good. The man was a woman's dream come true.

A dream that was suddenly real. He was wearing jeans and a white shirt, open at the neck. Normally she would have checked the weave of the cotton, and the fit of his jeans, but she was too busy trying to catch her breath, and settle her racing heart.

She'd been concentrating so hard on dealing with her guilt over Yurii that she hadn't worked out a plan on how to deal with her feelings for Pierce. She'd been pushing them aside until she felt stronger. But he was here now, and he was sending her some very straightforward signals.

"Are you going to tuck tail and run, or see this thing through?" he asked.

"This thing?"

"Us."

The word had her scrambling for a safety net. "Is there an us? I thought we were just two—"

"Don't give me that two ships passing in the night crap. We've been set on this course since Austria."

She took a step back. "I didn't like you in Austria."

He must have thought she was going to leave. He took hold of her hand and when he did, he noticed that she was no longer wearing Yurii's ring.

He brushed his thumb over her naked finger. "It was a tough mission. Let's get some air."

It was all happening too fast. She pulled her hand

free. "You get some air. I have to pack. I'm leaving in the morning."

"It wasn't just sex in New Orleans. We both know that. You might have loved the idea of Yurii's devoted obsession with you, but that's not what you're here trying to forget."

"You arrogant ass." Casmir headed for the elevator.

"Now there's the woman I know and love."

She heard the words, but she refused to stop. She heard him swear, knew he was coming after her. She sprinted to the elevator and ducked inside and hit the button. It closed just as he reached it.

She had her key in her door when she saw him at the end of the hall. He'd had to take the stairs four at a time to get there so quickly.

She opened the door and scrambled inside. Before she could close it, he was pushing his way in.

He reached for her and pulled her against him.

"You're hurting me. I was shot, remember?"

"I remember. You took that bullet for me." He let her go. "Maybe I shouldn't have come."

He headed for the door.

"That's right, walk away. Go home."

He turned around. "I don't have a home. Petrov burned it down."

"I'm sorry about that. The cabin was starting to grow on me."

"Like fungus, right?"

"You know me too well."

"My point. I know you, and what you need. A

man who really loves you. The spy as well as the woman with the silver lining."

Casmir's heart started to pound. "And you think you're that man?"

"*Oui.* I know I'm that man."

"I don't know what to say."

"That would be a first." He walked back to her and slipped his arm around her and drew her close. "But you don't have to say anything. That look says it all. I'm your man, *amant.* Take whatever you need from me. You know I am."

"You think I love you?"

"Do you?"

"Yes. Oh, God, what's Mama going to say?"

"I stopped off in Santo Domingo on my way here. She told me to tell you to follow your heart and…"

"And?"

"And Lazie gave me a piece of advice, too."

Casmir arched her eyebrows. "I can hardly wait to hear."

"He told me not to let you out of bed for a week."

"Are you planning on taking his advice?"

"*Oui.* Starting right now."

"Before you do, I need to equal the playing field. If you remember, I owe you a kiss."

She curled her arms around his neck, and pressed her lips against his. The kiss was long and deliberate, full of passion.

Pierce ran his hands slowly over her hips and cupped her ass. Pulling her against him, he kissed her back.

The moment was powerful and heartfelt. It melted the bitch, turned on the woman, and Casmir kicked off her shoes.

* * * * *

*Coming in summer 2006
to Silhouette Intimate Moments,
don't miss Wendy Rosnau's next book
in her SPY GAMES miniseries,
UNDERCOVER NIGHTINGALE.*

*Super chills and sexy thrills abound
at Silhouette Bombshell!
We're your destination for the best in women's
romantic action-adventure stories.
Turn the page for a sneak peek at one of next
month's releases,*

DAUGHTER OF THE FLAMES
by Nancy Holder

*Available June 2006
wherever Silhouette Books are sold.*

"Isabelle!"

Izzy's eyes flew open at the sound of a male voice in her room.

She knew that voice. It was one of the men who had appeared in her dream—the second one, in the monastery, with the wild hair tumbling over his shoulders and smoke rising up behind him. The one whom she had answered, in French.

She started fumbling for the light, but she was in a strange room, and she didn't know where it was.

"C'est moi, Jean-Marc de Devereaux des Ombres."

His voice was insistent, urgent. But it was inside her head. *In her mind.*

Oh, my God. What's going on?

Was she dreaming?

"You're in danger," he said.

Experimentally, she touched her head, feeling for headphones. Patting the pillow. "Who are you?" she demanded again, squinting into the darkness. "Where are you?"

"A friend. Trust me. They're looking for you."

I've gone crazy, she thought. But as she looked around again, she said hopefully, "Ma?"

"No, I'm not Marianne. But I speak for her. I speak for the House of the Flames. They're searching for you. I'll do all I can to protect you."

Suddenly a violent pain blossomed behind her eyes. With a gasp, she pressed her fingertips against the bridge of her nose. It was so bad that she doubled over, losing her balance, and tumbled on her knees to the floor.

"Did you do that?" she yelled.

"Shh. Lower your voice. They know where you are. But they're closing in."

Holding on to her bed, she got to her feet. The pain disappeared. Rubbing her forehead, she saw a rectangle of light around Venetian blinds. She stood to the side of it, then lifted the corner of the dark-blue curtain and spied out onto the street below.

Her heart turned to ice.

The first man from her dream, the one in the long black coat, stood across the street. He was smoking; she saw the glow of his cigarette against the dark outline of his head. He was not looking at her window; his gaze was focused a floor or two above it. But he was searching, scanning. She felt the familiar, irrational dread at the sight of him.

She murmured, "Is that you or a friend of yours?"

"Is someone outside?"

"Yes," she said.

"Get out! Get out immediately. Don't let him see you or you are dead."

"Okay, wait. Time out," she said. "What the hell is going on?"

"Maintenant! Vite!"

"I have to get dressed—"

"Non! Get out! Get out now! Move!"

Something inside her made her listen—she had saved her father's life this way—and she whipped into action, bounding across the room to the chair where she had piled her clothes.

"Get out now!"

She gathered up her sweater and pants, stepped into her boots, and pulled on her own long black coat over the Marc Anthony T-shirt. Her purse...she couldn't remember where it was. In the darkened bedroom? In the bathroom?

She couldn't leave without it. Her cell phone was in it. Her money, her house key—

And then she felt the wet velvet sensation wash over her, the same as in her bathroom—was it four nights ago? She stood stock-still, feeling like a prisoner eluding the searchlight of a prison guard tower. Her heart was thudding so hard she felt dizzy again.

The sensation passed.

"*Where are you?*" the voice demanded. "*Are you leaving?*"

"*Oui,*" she replied, shocking herself. She was speaking in French again.

"*Ah, c'est bon,*" he replied, and rattled off a barrage of French.

She shook her head, not understanding anything more, mincing backward out of the bedroom.

There, in the living room, her purse lay on the sofa turned upside down.

She grabbed it up, scooping the contents in as best she could, and hurried to the front door. She opened the door and went out into the hall, shutting it behind herself.

"*Move! Or others will die!*"

The words chilled her. They were straight from her nightmare.

"Where? Where should I go?" she whispered, since it didn't seem to matter how softly or how loudly she spoke. "How can you hear me? What's going on?"

"*Just go!*"

As soundlessly as she could, she crept down the hall, which was dark except for a light flickering dimly in front of the elevator. Bad move to take it, she decided.

It began to whir. It was coming up.

She looked frantically for a stairwell. Thought about what she might find there—junkies, bored gangbangers, eager thieves.

She made out the shape of a door and tiptoed

toward it, felt for a latch, found it and opened the door. She took a deep breath as she stepped across the threshold. It was pitch-dark.

Closing the door soundlessly behind herself, she had a moment of vertigo. It was so dark. She was so scared. She fumbled in her purse for her cell phone to call 911.

"Isabelle?" It was the voice inside her head. She didn't dare answer.

The elevator dinged. Though she knew she had no way of knowing who was in the elevator, she started down, hand in her purse. Her heart caught as she came up empty on her cell phone. She began to wonder if she had left it on the couch.

How many flights of stairs? She was wobbly. Her head hurt. Her hands were trembling and she was afraid her knees were going to buckle. She gripped the banister, which was metal…and sticky. She recoiled, rubbing her hand on the clothes cradled in her arm.

She heard the door above her open.

"Isabelle?" The voice inside her head was frantic. *"Répondez-moi! Answer me!"*

There were footsteps on the stairs.

She held on to the banister again, moving as quietly as she could, wondering if speed was more important. Her heart rammed against her ribs; she was holding her breath and she couldn't make herself let it go. Her body went numb; she had no idea where her hand ended and the banister began.

Down she raced, each movement a cannonball

to her ears—she had no idea if the other person on the stairs could hear her. Part of her wanted to burst into hysterical laughter; the other part remembered that her father had almost died today and either she—or her mother's angelic spirit— had saved him.

Now someone was trying to save her.

Or was he trying to flush her out so someone else could catch her?

She turned a corner, raced down more stairs.

The footsteps above her picked up speed.

She went around another corner. Another.

The footsteps above her rang out, obviously not caring if she heard them.

As she turned another corner, she saw a horizontal sliver of light at an angle below her. It was light from beneath a door. It had to be coming in from somewhere—a service tunnel? A stoop?

Someone's flashlight?

She looked up and over her shoulder. Saw no one.

Looked back down at the strip of light.

The voice inside her head starting yelling her name.

"Isabelle! Isabelle! Isabelle!"

She pushed open the door and just as quickly shut it behind herself, feeling along the latch for a way to lock it. There was none.

She wheeled around on a square of cement and stared out on a strip of snow bounded by two privacy fences. There was a six-foot-high fence at the other end.

She stepped into the snow. It went up to her calf, and the cold was a shock. She rethought her plan. She was practically naked, and every movement she made would be a roadmap to her location.

She had no other choice.

She put her other foot into the snow.

Four sisters.
A family legacy.
And someone is out to destroy it.

A captivating new limited continuity, launching June 2006

The most beautiful hotel in New Orleans,
and someone is out to destroy it. But mystery,
danger and some surprising family revelations
and discoveries won't stop the Marchand sisters
from protecting their birthright...
and finding love along the way.

**Hidden in the secrets of antiquity,
lies the unimagined truth...**

Introducing

a brand-new line filled with mystery
and suspense, action and adventure,
and a fascinating look into history.

And it all begins with DESTINY.

In a sealed crypt in
France, where the
terrifying legend of
the beast of Gevaudan
begins to unravel,
Annja Creed discovers
a stunning artifact
that will seal her destiny.

*Available every other
month starting
July 2006, wherever
you buy books.*

GRA1